Through Bitter Seasons

by Jean Springer

Cover Illustration by Brenda Mann

Dedicated with understanding
to all the Elizabeths
who struggle with the paralysis of bitterness,
and to all the Jonases
who are used by the Lord
to free them.

One

The voice of the pilot over the intercom and the braking power of the small jet plane pulling her forcefully out of the seat brought Elizabeth Thurston from an hour of difficult memories to exciting reality.

Eagerly, she laid aside pencil and sketch pad and peered out the window to catch a glimpse of magnificent palm trees, patterned rice fields, and hundreds of tall temple spirals thinly penciling the late afternoon sky. She smiled as she caught sight of a modern golf course hugging one edge of the airport while teakwood-bodied trucks jammed a loading zone and small, brightly painted cabs waited to make profitable fares on those passengers recently deplaned.

"So you've finally gotten excited about something," a man's deep voice lazily teased her.

Quickly dampening her animation and erasing any emotion from her face, Elizabeth turned from the window to face her interrogator.

Jonas Adams, a ruggedly handsome, successful business-man, and her brother's new employer, flipped open his seat belt with the casualness of a seasoned traveler. He flexed his long legs, slipped the jacket of his pale blue tropical suit on over wide shoulders and grinned at her reserved expression. She turned away from his keen brown eyes to gather her things together, determined to ignore his observation.

"I was beginning to think you were regretting this trip," he said lightly, one hand smoothing back unruly black hair that often fell over his forehead. His manner was warm and genial because he was gregarious by nature, but he watched the young woman carefully. Her coral sleeveless dress was cool and practical and its cheery brightness mocked her solemnity. She was steeling herself to remain impassive to his friendliness, and he wondered why.

She had a tall, willowy model's figure, light brown hair cut short in the latest fashion, and a narrow photogenic face with a perfect smile. He, however, had not been awarded even one of those smiles since the beginning of their association in Los Angeles two weeks previous. Pure blue eyes, too often flashing scorn at any man other than her brother, sparkled with pleasure only when she thought she was unobserved.

Whatever had been troubling her during the commercial flight from Los Angeles to Singapore had made her seem particularly vulnerable, and the unaffected charm he saw in unguarded moments only intensified Jonas Adams' interest. The fact that he was ten years older than Elizabeth bothered him not one bit, nor that he had only known her two weeks. It was obvious that she needed a friend, someone to take care of her, and he felt he was just the one to do it.

She persistently kept her brother Martin between them like a buffer zone, but Jonas was aware of her inner tension. She had built quite a indomitable barrier that snubbed any offer of friendship, and hid her true nature to all but her brother. Adams had seen her in a relaxed mood with Martin, full of charm and happiness and laughter, only to watch her turn cold and silent toward him. This display of cynicism was completely at odds with her vocational prospects in Bangkok; it would kill any loving service she expected to have among the Thai.

The flight from Singapore to Bangkok had provided his first opportunity to be alone with her and he had not pushed too hard for any response. Nor had he gotten any, at least none that was favorable.

"If I can help you in any way, Elizabeth, just let me know." It was a loaded statement, one calculated to get some kind of comment, and he watched her with interest.

She glanced forward to where her brother sat at one of the controls, obviously wishing for his interceding presence, then shook her head stubbornly. "Thanks, but please don't trouble yourself on my account." Her voice was as cool as the smile that did not quite reach her eyes. He grinned knowingly when she quickly changed the subject. "I'm happy to be back in Thailand and it's going to be great surprising my parents by arriving three weeks earlier than they expected. Mr. Adams . . ."

"My name is Jonas."

Wary and cautious against any unwanted familiarity, Elizabeth caught his expression of congenial amusement and felt her cheeks grow warm with embarrassment and anger. He probably thought she was a foolish little school girl, completely lacking in poise and confidence.

She hesitated, clasping the sketch pad tightly and quelling the urge to inform him that there wasn't a man on earth with whom she cared to establish any sort of friendly relationship, and if she chose not to use his first name, that was her prerogative.

Ignoring his interruption, she continued. "Mr. Adams, I want to thank you for inviting us to travel with you. It's saved so much time, not to mention expense." She frowned at his raised eyebrows and said stiffly, "I'm afraid you're going to spoil us both."

"That might be a pleasure I can't afford to pass up," he replied nonchalantly, feeling her eye him suspiciously. He tossed several papers he had been studying into a briefcase on the seat next to him and clicked it shut.

"I'm sure Martin will do an excellent job of flying me around Southeast Asia, so I'll be repaid many times over."

Elizabeth glanced down at the gold embossed signature on the briefcase—*Adams Export, Ltd.*—and nodded. If Martin were responsible for keeping up with his new boss, he would indeed be a busy pilot.

And being a pilot was what he had always wanted. For as long as she could remember, Martin had been fascinated by airplanes. His dorm room at the mission school in the mountains had been filled with all types of models, and he and his chums spent many happy hours trying to fly homemade planes and space ships.

Rather than be involved in tribal work with his parents as he had once planned, he came to the conclusion he could be more effective in sharing his Christian faith in the business world, and in his own efficient and practical manner had set a quiet but determined course in that direction. He had finished college ahead of Elizabeth and took an extra year of flight training. Now they were back in Thailand and in a day or two would travel up-country into the mountains to visit their parents.

Afterward, Martin would be flying for Jonas' company and Elizabeth would begin a job in the programming department of a Christian radio station in Bangkok. Martin had reached his goal, but hers had disappeared suddenly and she was still adjusting, taking this assignment as a temporary measure until she knew what she was to do.

She sighed unconsciously and brushed her short brunette

hair away from her face. In all of the emotional upheaval she had just been through, Martin's easy-going, steady influence had been a gift from God, a port in the storm for her.

The plane taxied to a full stop, the motors died, and the door opened. Elizabeth reached for her shoulder bag and sketch pad and as she stood, felt Jonas' hand under her elbow, guiding her firmly down the aisle to the door.

She caught her breath at the wave of hot air engulfing them as they walked down the waiting steps to the cement runway and murmured, "I'd forgotten how hot it can be, even during the rainy season."

"You'll get acclimatized again, but I hope you'll take it easy for a few weeks. Don't try to keep the same kind of schedule you did back in the States. Life here is much slower and easier, as you well know."

They turned toward the air terminal and Elizabeth heard Martin walking behind them in deep conversation with the co-pilot, and knew she was to spend more time alone with the man beside her.

He was aware of this also, and being an astute businessman who seizes every opportunity, thought he would press his advantage and make another attempt at reaching the girl beside him. Casting a perceptive glance at her cool profile, he began.

"Liz . . ." He felt her censured look at his use of Martin's pet name but went on. "Liz, what's troubling you? Are you worried about your job at the radio station?"

At the negative response he saw, he probed further. "About Martin?" Another shake of the head. "Well, something has been bothering you this entire trip, what is it?"

"How do you know? You've only known me this trip."

"It's quite obvious. Come on, tell me."

Elizabeth caught her breath in exasperation and came to

an abrupt stop. Looking him straight in the eye she spoke in a voice full of hurt and anger.

"You've been waiting for two weeks to get at me, haven't you? I've felt you watching me like . . . like some . . . sleek cat waiting to pounce on its prey!" She took a deep breath, tightened her lips and then said softly, "All right, if you're so anxious to know. I was engaged to a man who suddenly decided he could not waste his talents in a foreign country. He was offered a lucrative position with a national broadcasting company and . . ."

She stopped, finding it almost impossible to finally voice the words that had been repeating themselves over and over in her mind.

"And?" he prodded.

She fought back sudden angry tears and said reluctantly, "And, he . . . he delivered an ultimatum on graduation night. If I persisted in coming to Thailand the engagement was off, permanently. Now are you satisfied?"

Jonas stared down at her unhappy face and whistled softly. "And so, you've decided no man is to be trusted."

They stood in the charged silence, staring at one another, waiting for the two pilots to side-step them and continue on toward the door of the building marked "Flight Personnel Only."

Elizabeth spoke first, her voice biting and caustic, her blue eyes sparkling up at him: "How dare you talk to me like that!"

"Of course I dare. I'm your friend, whether you want it that way or not, and I'm not going to let you turn into an embittered woman because one foolish young man failed to put Christ first in his life."

"Are you judging him?" she queried, feeling the need to be defensive.

"Are you defending him?" he countered.

She gasped as he spoke and turned sharply away, but his

hand on her arm restrained her hurried steps and he said, "O.K. I'll admit that I don't know what God wants him to do with his life, but I do know you won't be worth a Thai dollar to the Lord if you let this eat away at you."

Staring unseeingly at the grey ribbon of sidewalk passing beneath their feet, she tried to pull away from his hold but succeeded only in dropping her sketch pad, which fell open to the picture of a young man heavily marked through with dark, angry lines.

Jonas scooped it up from the pavement, deliberately turning the picture toward her, and saw a look of dismay flash across her face as she stood silently staring at the sketch. Pulling it from his hand she asked defiantly, "And what makes you think I'm bitter?"

The answer came softly and was so full of kindness that her eyes went quickly to his face, then slid away again.

"That," he said, tapping the picture in her hand. "And, I've been watching you the past two weeks." She could hear amusement in his voice before he went on, "But not with the motives of a sleek cat." His eyes grew serious. "You haven't allowed anyone but Martin to get past that protective shell you've built."

He pushed open the door and followed her inside to a large, air-conditioned waiting room. She tried to ignore his presence but felt him close behind her.

"Just remember," he murmured, his voice low but emphatic, "it can be very lonely behind those walls."

Startled at his audacity, she followed him silently through the immigration line and then sank down gratefully on a cushioned bench while he put his briefcase on the floor by her feet.

Turning with a smile, he raised his hands, palms together and chest high, in the traditional Thai greeting, and spoke to three businessmen waiting for him. His conversation was in Thai and Elizabeth did not attempt to follow, but she could not take her eyes from his tall, lean figure. The pale blue suit contrasted smartly with dark hair and sun-tanned face, and judging from the response of those with him, he was respected and well-liked. As she watched, he stopped his conversation to laughingly and gently untangle his long legs from the persistent arms of a little olive-skinned, black-eyed boy. It was an action that touched her deeply, yet was perversely irritating.

She frowned, not willing to confess even a begrudging belief in Martin's praise of Jonas Adams' strength and gentleness, of his work on behalf of the poor, and of instances where he put himself and his business on the line in his desire that others know Christ as their Savior. In the few months of their association, Martin had developed an almost worshipful attitude toward his new employer. Elizabeth had commented on this once, but Martin only replied, "He's a solid as a rock, dynamic yet humble, and he makes you feel that you're the most important person in the world. He really cares." And when she had finally met the man two weeks ago, she was ready to dislike him because of what had just taken place in her life.

Elizabeth could not understand why she resented Jonas Adams, why his concern triggered her distrust and increased her determination to stay away from him. Nor could she understand why his offer of help angered her so. But he was like an abrasion to her bruised emotions.

She had to admit that he was right about her attitude. He had drilled with the precision of a dentist to the root of the problem by forcing her to face the truth. She was allowing bitterness to eat away her joy and usefulness to God. One disappointment, no matter how difficult, shouldn't shipwreck her life.

Standing head and shoulders over most of the Asians in the room, Jonas had only to look up to keep her in view. And each time their eyes met, the message was the same—

he wasn't finished with her yet.

It was a kindly warning. The tension grew and knotted her stomach, and her fretful eyes darted around the room in search of Martin. Why wasn't he with her now, so that he could stand between her and this forceful man who seemed bent on dominating her life? The dismay she suddenly felt at the possibility of becoming entangled in another highly-charged relationship was enough to bring her surging to her feet with the intention of finding Martin and getting away from Jonas Adams as soon as she possibly could.

And just as quickly, Jonas glanced up, his dark, compelling eyes pinning her gaze until she reluctantly sank down again on the bench. It was a silly thing for her to do anyway, for she had no idea where she would find Martin. Another look from Jonas told her that he knew what she was contemplating. Shrugging her shoulders as though it would break his stare, she deliberately turned to look with keen interest at the bustling excitement in the room. With outbursts in many languages, it was a noisy river of international activity.

A group of tourists, all wide-eyed and talking, and all obviously American if one could judge by the profuse number of cameras, were being patiently herded toward the front entrance by an attractive young Thai woman. She wore a tour guide's uniform of blue skirt, white blouse and a perky blue cap, which accentuated beautiful, coal-black hair done in a smart style.

A harrassed Chinese mother tried to comfort her crying infant while keeping up with an inquisitive, round-faced little toddler. Several Hindu businessmen with turbaned heads and expensive business suits strolled by, gesturing wildly and talking vociferously.

She felt someone brush her arm as they walked by, and as she turned to see who it was, she noticed an envelope lying on the seat next to her. After scanning the people nearby to find that none of them seemed the least bit interested in her, she picked up the envelope, feeling a bit foolish—for someone could be playing a practical joke, though that did not seem likely in Thailand. She glanced at Jonas, but his head was lowered as he listened to the conversation about him. Half hiding the envelope under her purse, she pulled out a one-page, typewritten note and her eyes widened in surprise. It was a warning of terrible trouble about to descend upon the reader, signed ominously by the "Red Tiger"! Quickly, she glanced around again, but no one was looking her way.

Jonas had not noticed her yet, so in great anger she ripped the note in half and tossed it into an ultra-modern waste bin nearby. How ridiculous, she thought, and not worth a moment's worry.

But where was Martin? She glanced around, still angry with the note, and there was Martin, ambling slowly across the room, enjoying the atmosphere and in no hurry to leave.

It wasn't difficult to see they were related, both having the same features, the same brown hair and blue eyes. He adjusted his wire-rimmed glasses with a characteristic gesture that was so familiar, and smiled at Elizabeth.

"Where have you been?" she asked sharply, wondering if she should mention the note, and then deciding it wasn't important.

He raised his eyebrows inquiringly at the anxiety in her voice and replied patiently, "Patterson was giving me last-minute instructions. He leaves for California as soon as he brings Jonas back from this trip to India and I won't have a chance to talk with him again. He's been very helpful."

"When do they leave?" Soon, she hoped. She wanted to regain her equilibrium away from the all-seeing eyes of Mr. Jonas Adams.

Glancing down at her tightly clenched hands, Martin replied, "Late this evening, I think."

Deciding it best to change the subject, he began talking of their immediate plans—what they would do before leaving for the north and whether or not they would be able to contact their parents the next day. He suggested a visit to the Grand Palace or the floating markets.

"I'm looking forward to seeing the city again, aren't you, Liz?"

"Martin," she said impatiently, "what are we waiting for? Can't we go to the hotel now?"

"You haven't heard a word I've said, Liz. Something troubling you?"

Seeing her glance quickly at Jonas, he remembered hearing part of their heated discussion while walking into the terminal and wisely chose not to press the issue. It would come to light soon enough.

In the meantime, he was interested to see an agitated young Thai join the group around Jonas. Dresses in white shirt and navy blue trousers, with straight black hair and dark eyes, he was slightly taller than usual for his nationality and seemed to be an employee of the tall American.

"Well, it looks as though a problem has hit the business world," Martin noted casually to Elizabeth.

They watched the young man talking earnestly, punctuating his information with the Asian manner of pointing—a thrust of the chin—in their direction. Apparently, they were being discussed. When the young man had completed his report, Jonas made several comments, said good-bye to the businessmen, and then continued his discussion with the young man, who then handed him an envelope. Elizabeth saw the displeased frown on Jonas' face as he read the message, tucked the paper back into the envelope and put it in his coat pocket. He gave some instructions to the young man and then brought him over to the bench.

"Elizabeth, Martin, this is Damrong, my Bangkok manager and very capable assistant. Damrong—Elizabeth and Martin Thurston."

"*Sawat dee krap.* Welcome to Thailand." Damrong shook hands with Martin and turned to greet Elizabeth with the traditional Thai greeting, as she had seen Jonas do earlier. His dark eyes sparkled, his interest wholly taken up with the attractive young woman before him.

"Miss Thurston, I hope you will allow me to show you Bangkok while you are here," he added, still staring at Elizabeth, his friendly smile compelling one from her.

Martin sneaked a look at his employer and grinned slightly. Jonas was watching his handsome manager charm Elizabeth into the happiest attitude he had probably seen, and was undoubtedly unaware that she did not feel as threatened by Damrong as she surely did with him. This had all the signs of being an interesting situation and one which Martin would enjoy observing. He had no fears that his new employer would ever be as unkind to his sister as her fiance had been.

He heard Elizabeth ask if Damrong's exceptional command of the English language came from studying in England.

"Yes, I spent four years there and two in America, where I met Mr. Adams. I am most western in my way of life now."

"Almost, but not quite," Jonas remarked dryly. evidently deciding this had gone far enough. "Damrong, tell me more of what's been happening."

"The warning note is the third one . . ."

Jonas stopped him with a touch on the arm. "No, Damrong, I was asking about the martial law."

Elizabeth and Martin exchanged glances. What

warnings had been received and was Jonas Adam's life in danger? She wanted to ask if it was the same letter she had just thrown away, but Damrong was talking.

"There have been rumors of some *farang* who are making trouble for the government. It is mostly young people who come to Thailand looking for free living and drugs," he said apologetically. "They have been stirring up student unrest and some riots, and there has been talk of another coup. That is why martial law was declared today. Every *farang* must show the passport at any time or be put into jail immediately. We heard that two were killed by the military only yesterday in a small town not far from Bangkok. No trial, no questions—just shot."

"Oh, how horrible," Elizabeth said, shuddering not for herself, for she had no need to be anxious, she thought, but for the two unfortunate foreigners.

Jonas turned to Martin and shook his head. "You must be careful. If you're caught without your passports you might not have opportunity to explain." He paused and frowned his way through a decision. "I'm not sure I should let you travel up-country now."

Elizabeth's blue eyes widened expressively and her mouth flew open to register an objection to his interfering ways, but he had already turned to another matter.

"Damrong, has our luggage gone through customs?"

"Yes, I saw to it myself and it is loaded in the van."

"Thanks." Jonas picked up his briefcase and helped Elizabeth to her feet.

"My cassette tapes weren't taken, were they, Damrong?" Elizabeth had recorded Thai melodies to bring to the radio station and was relieved to hear the the customs inspector had removed nothing from her luggage.

"A Thai student and I spent hours adapting hymns to Thai melodies. It would be a disaster if those tapes didn't get to the station."

It was not until they had maneuvered slowly through most of the crowd that Elizabeth realized there was a definite possessiveness in Jonas' touch as he guided her nearer the doorway and she looked up suspiciously. But he squelched any protest as his fingers tightened warningly on her arm, just as though he knew her thoughts. He really was taking quite a lot for granted, Elizabeth thought, and felt she would soon tell him so.

A spark of anger flared in her eyes, then died as quickly as it had come as two military police stepped forward to halt their progress. Shining brass, colorful braid-decorated sleeves and caps, smart khaki uniforms without a wrinkle, guns strapped to their hips—they did not appear at all friendly when they spoke first to Martin and Damrong.

"Your passport, Liz." The quiet confidence in Jonas' voice calmed her sudden fluttering nerves as she quickly placed it in his outstretched hand.

Two

Not long afterward, she sat looking out of the van window as Damrong negotiated the heavy airport traffic, her mind on what she had just seen. Absentmindedly, she began sketching two figures on the pad in her lap, fingers moving confidently as she thought over the scene with the police.

There had been an instant change of attitude when Jonas opened his passport and spoke to the two men in their own language. Surely he wasn't known by all the military police in the large, sprawling city of Bangkok! She was not easily fearful, but these warnings and the martial law business were a little unnerving to face on their first day back in Thailand, and she supposed she was making too much of Jonas' influence.

From the front seat of the van, Martin turned to glance back at his sister, thinking she was unusually still. "Who are you sketching, Liz?"

She was startled from her thoughts and laughed ruefully. "I really must break this habit, but I'm not even aware of doing it."

"Someone at the airport?" Jonas pulled the pad gently from her hands and studied the sketch of two young people with interest. He had discarded his coat and tie, and with his white shirt darkening his tan, he seemed a little more threatening to Elizabeth.

Her response was a curt "Yes, as a matter of fact, it is. They caught my eye as we were talking with the police. I only noticed them because I felt someone staring at me."

"Yes, I saw them also." There was amusement and mock despair in Jonas' voice then. "You're going to miss too much of this twenty-mile trip into Bangkok if you keep this up. "I'll hold on to this,"—he indicated the sketch pad—"until we get to my house."

"Your house? Why are we going there?"

"I don't want you and Martin staying at the hotel with . . ." He glanced at Damrong and then continued, ". . . with all this trouble in the city." His voice sounded too dogmatic to suit Elizabeth.

"No," she declared emphatically. Then glancing at Martin, she lowered her voice but said decisively, "I don't want to stay in your house. I have been looking forward to spending my first night back in Bangkok in the Hotel of the Beautiful Palms. We've been there before and I like it. There's no reason for us to go to your home. Besides, I'm sure your housekeeper isn't prepared for company."

"My housekeeper is away right now, so . . ."

"So," she interrupted triumphantly, "you see. We shouldn't go there at all."

"Why not? Can't you cook?" Jonas' teasing smile angered her further, but she checked her reply to his question.

She was quickly learning that it was useless to argue with him once his mind was made up, but taking a deep breath, she forced any anger from her voice and said pleadingly,

"Please, let us stay at the hotel. Please?"

"My, my, Liz. I'm hurt. Don't you want to see what my house is like?"

"I . . ." She quickly swallowed the sharp retort hovering on her tongue. "I would, but not tonight. I want to see the beautiful garden at the hotel and have some fried rice and curry, and sit on that wide veranda and watch the people in the little shops, and . . ."

Jonas threw up his hand in mock surrender. "I give up. You win—but against my better judgment. Martin, never let it be said that the female of the species is without persuasive weapons."

Turning to Elizabeth he caught the triumphant look she flashed at Martin and asked wryly, "You . . . actress. Would you have tried tears next?"

Unable to restrain herself, even though it might mean losing this unexpected victory, Elizabeth asked in disbelief, "Would tears have the slightest effect on you?"

"Only if they were honest ones."

She was surprised by the sincerity of his reply, and silently watched him study the sketch of the two young people she had just done.

The girl's face, scowling and sullen, was framed by long, straight hair. The young man, timid and even a little frightened, stared from the page through wire-framed glasses similar to Martin's.

"You do a great job of catching expressions and emotions, Liz. You have a degree in art, don't you?"

Elizabeth retreated into her shell again at Jonas' compliment and answered more curtly than she should have. "Yes, I do." She turned away from any more discussion of her abilities and looked out the window.

It was raining now. A soft, silent, tropical rain that landed gently but persistently down on the green paper umbrellas of those who walked along the roadside or plodded across the pathways bordering the rice paddies. Others guided their bicycles with one hand and held up a protective umbrella with the other, adroitly dodging pedestrains, animals and water puddles with an unshaken carelessness. The *klongs*—the canals of Thailand—were filled to overflowing with the rainy season's endeavors, but in the months ahead some would be completely dry and unuseable as a water highway.

From the silence Damrong had maintained throughout this last exchange between his employer and the pretty young American, he was evidently planning not only a neutral position, but at least outwardly, meant to ignore what had been said.

His first attempts at conversation came after he had sounded a long blast of the horn, warning two capricious taxies to stay out of his traffic lane, and he questioned Martin about the English expression, "Is it 'each man for his own?' " It seemed a fitting thought applied to the intense driving of his fellow countrymen.

"I believe you mean 'every man for himself.' It's an expression that always reminds me of a sentence in the Bible," Martin replied.

"And what is that?" Damrong asked with interest.

"During the time of the judges in Israel, the people kept repeating cycles of sin . . ."

"What is cycles of sin?" Damrong interrupted, keeping his eye on the heavy traffic ahead.

"Cycle means repeating, doing something again and again. The people kept sinning, receiving God's punishment and being restored. This happened again and again. At the end of the book of Judges there's a statement which says 'every man did that which was right in his own eyes.' "

"You believe there is a . . .," Damrong hesitated, hunting the English word he wanted, "a connection between sinning and doing what they thought was right?"

"Yes, I do. Let's say a man decided it was right for him to kill anyone he wanted, for whatever reason he had; he would, in the end, be punished."

"But Jesus was killed—what did He do?"

"He did no wrong, but took the punishment we deserve for our sins, so that we might have God's forgiveness and salvation."

Damrong shot a quick, approving glance at Martin. "I think you would like to come to the evening Bible study, yes? It is in English and Thai."

"Yes, I'd like to, whenever I'm in Bangkok." Martin motioned toward an entire block of buildings. "Those look new. I don't remember this area being so developed the last time I was here."

"Buildings go up all the time. That block is full of new apartments—all small, hot and crowded." Damrong flashed a quick smile and shook his head. "I prefer my parent's home, a true Thai house built up off the ground, open and cool. Those little shops," he pointed with a jut of the chin, "have been there a long time, as long as I can remember. One of them has excellent Thai silk. Your sister might like some, yes?"

Elizabeth turned her head slightly to sneak a look at Martin, knowing they both had the same thought—Damrong had just issued a subtle hint of interest in her. Her brother's face was unreadable but she saw the merriment in his eyes and frowned, warning him with a look that he had better not encourage Damrong.

But Martin had no intention of doing anything. He settled back, much as a spectator at a play, to see what would happen next. It was now time, he thought, for Jonas to make a move.

And he did. Clearing his throat, Jonas spoke to Damrong. "How is the train service up-country? They aren't flooded out yet, are they?"

"The trains were running yesterday, but we expect that is the last time for about a week."

"Check it again tomorrow, please, and see if you can get a telegram through to the mission in Chiangmai, in case word can be sent up the mountain to the Thurstons. I'm sure they would like to know that Elizabeth and Martin are here. And since the service isn't too good, I'd appreciate it if you'd handle this for Martin."

"Right. Tomorrow, I will see what can be done."

"Good." Jonas chewed his lower lip in frustration as he flipped a page in the sketchbook. "If I could cancel this trip to India, we'd fly up to Chiangmai." He was uneasy about leaving, but did not want Elizabeth to know just how concerned he really felt. The three anonymous letters were serious threats to his business and employees, and he was also responsible for this brother and sister. He had instructed Damrong to contact the police, and to try to look out for the Thurstons, but otherwise his hands were tied.

As he flipped the next page, he and Elizabeth reacted simultaneously to the book in his hands. There was an amused "Ah ha" from him and a horrified whisper of "Oh, no!" from her as she suddenly remembered one of her sketches.

Quickly she reached for the pad, berating herself for forgetting about the picture, but felt a strong hand close around her wrist and heard him say quietly, "It's too late. I've already seen it."

Elizabeth sighed, unhappy that he had found the sketch done in black, harsh lines, but resigned herself to the impending line of fire she felt sure was coming. She sat back and watched his face, tugging all the while to be released from his grasp, which only tightened each time she pulled.

"Do I really look that severe?" His dark eyes glittered

with amusement, his face quite unlike the frowning, stern man with piercing eyes that she had drawn in a moment of anger.

"You're hurting my hand," she replied, looking down at his hand on hers.

"It wouldn't hurt if you would stop struggling," he said significantly, and smiled at the one final tug of defiance before her hand was stilled beneath his. She was aware that he was referring to her bitter attitude and frowningly turned to stare out at the rain-drenched scenes that were to become part of her life again.

It was raining harder now; a deluge. It slowed the traffic so that she was able to look into the shops. There were several Chinese men sitting in an open-front restaurant, looking placidly content as they patiently watched traffic; they would probably be on their way once the rain lessened.

She remembered one monsoon season when it rained four days straight. First a mist, then pouring out of the sky as though a dam had broken, and then a light drizzle; but it didn't stop once during those days. And this wasn't unusual for the rainy season. The reason it came to her now was that those four days had been holiday time with her parents and the constant rain had spoiled a few outdoor plans they had made. The local children never let it ruin theirs, however. They ran about in the rain and splashed in the puddles all they wanted.

At a question from Jonas she reluctantly consented to his request to study her work, and feeling her hand released, turned to watch him look over some sketches of children she had done while in Singapore.

He also praised a picture of her brother. "I like it," he added teasingly. "It doesn't have those black lines drawn through it."

There were several drawings of the Bangkok she had known as a child, and as he studied one of a canal crowded with small sampans, remarked that she would not see as many now. "Traffic has become so heavy that many of the canals have been filled in so that streets can be widened into four or six lanes. Your Bangkok will be changed; I hope you won't be disappointed."

"The hotel is the same, isn't it?" she asked hopefully. It would be a shame to have too many alterations on her first day in the country. There were pleasant recollections of holidays spent with her parents in that fine, old hotel. And perhaps, if she could relive them, she might regain her balance and shed her truculent feelings. What the hotel lacked in western modernization, it more than compensated for in true Thai atmosphere.

"You'll have to judge for yourself, Liz," Jonas answered. "Perhaps it won't be as grand as the one in your memory."

Elizabeth bristled at his friendly warning that pictures from the past were sometimes distorted. He was only being kind and she knew it, but still a perverse antagonism seeped into her mind. And it was startling to realize that it was becoming a common reaction toward men, especially toward this rugged, competent, caring one beside her. Her mind acknowledged the stupidity of putting everyone into the same mold with her former fiance, but the emotions of bitter resentment and strong skepticism seemed to run wild.

She heard Damrong talking to Martin about the changes in the city and there was a note of pride in the Thai's voice as he described how modern they had become.

"But," he admitted, "life in our country is still easygoing, especially in the countryside. And our people still gentle and peaceful. *Mai pen rai* remains our answer to most problems. *Mai pen rai*—never mind—if someone misses an appointment, simply make another. Never mind if someone gets in an embarrassing place, it will be better next time. It solves a lot of difficulties, don't you think?"

Elizabeth smiled and asked if the young people had changed and become more western.

"Yes, they are torn between the beauty and serenity of our ancestor's way of life and the desire to be modern. Many young women wear western clothes now, and a great many families would rather live in the hot apartment houses than in a traditional home which is built for cool comfort. But that is progress."

"I'm not so sure," Jonas murmured, still looking at her sketches.

"Look, Liz," Martin interrupted to point ahead. "There's the Victory Monument."

She caught a glimpse of the memorial to the country's war dead before they turned on to Rajdamri Road. In a few minutes they were passing Lumpini Park. Damrong made a sharp turn into a narrow road and braked quickly to avoid smashing into a modern *samlor,* a three-wheeled motorized pedicab, which had carelessly pulled out into the road in front of them.

One more block, and then he turned the van into a long, curved driveway which was lined on both sides with stately palm trees and led up to the entrance of their hotel. Elizabeth leaned forward eagerly for a sweeping look over the gardens and building and found her memory materializing before her eyes. Everything looked the same, right down to the covered entrance where Damrong stopped the van and jumped out to help with the luggage.

Martin turned to her as they stood on the long wooden veranda, waiting for Jonas and Damrong. "Does it satisfy you?" he asked gently.

"Oh, yes. It's just as I remembered. I hope the rooms look the same, too."

"They are," Jonas said, moving to her side. "High ceiling fans, mosquito nets over the beds, very austere furnishings. I still think you should give up this idea. But, since you're so adamant, we'll get everything arranged and have supper here."

And without waiting for her approval, he did exactly that. Martin and Damrong carried luggage in while Jonas spoke to the manager, signed the register and then picked up Elizabeth's suitcase that sat at her feet. Before she had time to scarcely glance at the lobby, he was escorting her down the long, narrow hallway to the back of the hotel where their rooms were situated. He unlocked the door, and waited for her to enter before turning to hand Martin the key to the adjoining room.

Setting her luggage down beside the door and pointing to one opposite the desk, he said, "That door leads to Martin's room. I'll go and get a table in the dining room. You and Martin may want to freshen up a bit." He stepped back into the hallway to meet Damrong who was just coming out of Martin's room.

Elizabeth laid her purse and sketch pad on the desk and turned to take a long look at her new surroundings. The brown shades of the rattan furniture, the highly polished wood floor, and the soft, plain white cover on the bed looked very restful. There was a beautiful mirror framed in an intricate rattan pattern over the desk. The bed, with a mosquito net hanging over it from the ceiling, stood between the door to Martin's room and the outside wall. There was a long, barred window beside the bed that looked out onto the veranda which completely encircled the hotel. Two low-backed chairs stood in the other corner, and in front of them a low table, where she put her suitcase. Martin came through the connecting door to ask if she was ready for dinner.

"Just as soon as I wash up a little. Do you remember where the bathrooms are?"

"Down at the end of the hallway, I think." He looked down at his blue sport shirt, already damp with perspiration and decided he needed a clean one. "This heat will take some adjustment again."

Elizabeth pulled a wash cloth and towel from the rack hanging just to the right of her door and walked down the hallway to the bathroom where she let the cool faucet water run over her wrists and looked longingly at the white tiled shower stall. That would come later, she decided, when she had time to enjoy it.

After returning to her room, she pulled a cream-colored dress from her suitcase, gave it a shake and put it on, thinking that wrinkle-free materials were certainly a blessing. There was a light tap on the connecting door and she pulled it open to admit her brother as she walked to the mirror to run a comb through her hair. She wasn't trying to impress anyone, and didn't give her appearance much thought.

But others did. As she and Martin walked through the lobby to the dining room several men turned to look at the pretty young American. With her present distaste for most men, Elizabeth wasn't even aware of their stares.

Martin threw a questioning glance at Jonas and felt grateful for the thoughtful look the businessman gave his sister. Here was a man who would have a spiritual impact on her broken spirits, if only he could have enough contact with her. He was a busy man, with many responsibilities, but by the interest he was taking in Elizabeth, Martin felt that she was going to see more of him than she might expect. And it was bound to be a stormy relationship.

They were at the table only a moment before a waiter appeared with bowls of *Tom Yam Gung,* a special Thai soup, then plates of fried rice and curry, and afterwards, slices of pineapple, ripened before it was picked and tasting sweeter than any processed fruit ever could.

"I hope you are acclimatized enough for all this spicy food, Liz." Jonas shook his head at her appetite and asked how she could stay so thin.

Elizabeth didn't let his teasing bother her. "I've waited a long time for some food like this. It's so good!"

She listened to the men talk about the import business while she continued to enjoy the meal. Jonas was telling them that all of his employees were Christian; some before they began working for him, others under the influence of faithful, strong testimonies of the others.

He also spoke of the goal he had had ever since he first came to the city five years previously. "I want the Thais to see that a business can be run by Christian principles. They are so accustomed to 'tea money'—bribery—in order to get the most normal business transactions completed, and I refuse to do that. They hear us praying for every venture and see God providing answers. I'm also concerned that we help the poor and I feel I can do that by helping them become self-supporting through the small handicraft industries they have known for centuries. We've seen at least one hundred small home factories developed since I started the business."

He smiled as he poured more hot tea into their cups. "I've even had to preach a sermon or two while visiting up-country. My Thai isn't the best, but I study when I can."

"That was good food!" Martin sighed contentedly and sat back with a smile. "Jonas, what's the reaction from local businesses to your success?"

Jonas' glance at Elizabeth and then at Martin seemed to carry a cautious note, but his voice betrayed no concern. "A few are a little jealous, of course. But since I have the support of the government, and many influential friends," he shrugged his wide shoulders, "I'm tolerated. Those who dislike me realize they might have a small uprising on their hands if they tried to ruin my business. There are just too many people being helped financially and taking pride in themselves now."

"What about the warnings Damrong mentioned?" Martin asked.

Jonas rubbed his chin thoughtfully. "Someone has threatened to put me out of business, permanently."

"What will you do?" asked Elizabeth, slightly alarmed and remembering the note she had discarded.

"Nothing, except report it to the police. I can't spend all my time worrying about threats, even though this one has been repeated three times this week."

"These people you've been helping—is anything being done for them in a spiritual way?" There was a hint of irritation in Elizabeth's voice. It was as though she was trying to find a weak spot in Jonas' armor.

"Yes," came the quiet answer. "I've employed two full-time evangelists. And once someone has made a decision to follow Christ, we help them become involved in a local church."

Martin came to his defense with a casual question, while frowning slightly at his sister. "I've heard you're working with a clinic, too."

"We've started one in collaboration with an American mission here. It's primarily for my people, but many others are helped also."

Martin shot his sister a discerning look, then grinned at her uncomfortable expression. He decided to come to her rescue. "What shall we do tomorrow, Liz?"

"Well, if we can't get up-country for awhile, I'd love to see the house we used to live in, the floating markets in Thonburi, and the open-air market at the Phra Mane Grounds—for a start."

"For a start! Is that all?" Martin chuckled and shook his head. "I can see this is going to be a busy few days." Turning to his new employer, he asked, "Is there anything I can do for you before you leave?"

"Thanks, Martin. I can't think of anything now. I'm

going to postpone my India trip until tomorrow night, and I'd like to spend some time with you two. I'll pick you up in the morning and . . .''

"That's not necessary," Elizabeth interrupted suddenly. "Martin and I can manage quite well. I don't want you going out of your way for us."

"It's not out of the way. My home isn't too far from this hotel and it's just a block or two from my route into work. I'll pick you up about 7:30."

Both men expected a response from Elizabeth and when there was none, turned in surprise. She was staring out into the lobby where, from her place at the table, she could see the main desk.

"Liz?" Martin's voice was questioning. Surely she was going to protest Jonas' plan.

But Elizabeth was looking intently into the lobby. "If my eyes aren't deceiving me, those two young people at the desk are the same ones I sketched at the airport." She watched them talk with the desk manager and then her eyes widened a little as they looked straight at the place where she sat before they turned and hastily left the hotel.

"That's odd." She stood up. "Martin, I want to see where they're going."

Without waiting for the two men, she walked quickly through the lobby and out of the building, and looking to the left and right, saw no foreigners along the veranda. There was no one walking down the driveway, nor any movement around the vehicles parked along its edge.

The men had followed her sudden exit and Martin now stood beside her frowning. "What are you doing?" he asked mildly.

She felt Jonas beside her, but turned to speak to her brother. "Martin, it was the same two, I'm sure of it. And they looked straight in at me and then . . . left! Just as though they were checking up on us. I wonder why?"

"Are you sure?" Jonas asked, following her over to a long, cushioned bench, a little distance from the other hotel guests seated in the dim light of the porch.

"I'm sure."

"Let me have your sketchbook a minute, Liz. I'll check with the desk."

Surprised, she looked up into Jonas' face and saw that he was serious. In fact, more serious then she thought necessary. "It's . . . it's in my room, on my desk."

Martin stood up. "I'll get it."

In a few minutes Jonas stood with the sketchbook in his hand, showing the picture of the two young people to the man at the desk. The language was gradually coming back to Elizabeth and she understood the gist of his questioning. She watched the manager carefully for any unusual reaction, but he only seemed to be kind and helpful.

"They did ask if you and Martin were staying here at the hotel," Jonas informed them when they were once again sitting on the veranda. "They said that they thought you might be college friends, looked into the dining room, told the manager they were mistaken, and left."

He turned to look at Elizabeth seated next to him, and his expression triggered a streak of stubbornness that defied common sense.

"No," she said, anticipating his next sentence. "No, I want to stay here. What they said was probably true. I'm sure we won't see them again. It's not going to be a problem, is it, Martin?"

She glanced up at Martin, and then turned on Jonas. "Why do you think you can run my life? For goodness sake, stop being so bossy! *He's* your employee, not me!" Her gesture toward Martin made no impact upon the steady gaze she was receiving from Jonas, and deep inside she was afraid she had met her match. If Jonas was determined to move them from the hotel, he would; and she couldn't stop him without an embarrassing temper scene. She turned pleading eyes to her brother as he stood leaning against the veranda railing.

"Can't we go for a walk, Martin? I'd love to see the little shops along the road." She stood up, hoping he would take the hint, but saw him glance at Jonas and felt him receive a message. She was trapped when the tall businessman stood and reached for a hotel umbrella from the rack beside the bench.

"I'll go with you, Liz. Martin looks tired."

Taking the hint, Martin pulled his glasses off to rub his eyes wearily, and said, "I am getting sleepy, Liz. I'll go on to my room." He turned and strolled away, calling over his shoulder that he would leave the door open between their two rooms, in case she needed anything.

Elizabeth wanted to stamp her foot at him; he was so easy going, so ready to fall at Jonas' feet if asked. Would she ever see him get excited or upset about anything! Her sigh of annoyance brought a low chuckle from the man at her side.

"You aren't afraid to walk with me, are you, Liz?"

"I do wish you would stop calling me Liz! And no," she said, unconsciously straightening her shoulders, as though she were preparing for some distasteful task. "I'm not afraid of you."

"Good! Come on then, there's some pretty jewelry at one of those stores you might like to see."

Sharing the umbrella for protection against the light mist of the evening forced Liz to walk close to Jonas and produced a wish that she hadn't even mentioned the shops. And in the next moment, when his arm went lightly around her waist to guide her around a puddle of water, she wanted to turn and run—from even that friendly gesture. She had been hurt once by a man; she wasn't going to open herself up for it again—ever!

He must have felt her hesitation, for he looked down at her and smiled. "I'm not going to bite."

Then, without giving her an opportunity to reply, and with that hand still guiding her, he began talking about a new venture for his business.

"I would like to design a new catalog; one that would be bilingual—Thai and English—and would also have a definite Christian message. We have customers in many countries, such as England, South Africa, Canada, and America. It needs to be first class. And, I'd like to share my faith with the hundreds of customers who not only buy our items, but are interested in selling through our company as well."

He closed the umbrella and gave it a quick shake before following Elizabeth into the first small shop. "I want you to do the illustrations for me, Liz."

Elizabeth whirled around to face him in surprise. "Me?" she stammered. "Why me?"

Jonas turned to pick up a small, delicately-cut silver bracelet and answered, "I like your work."

"But aren't you using photography?"

"Yes, but I want some sketches illustrating the methods of production."

"You mean, showing a man hand-carving an animal or jewelry box from wood?"

"Exactly. We'll make some definite plans tomorrow when you come to my office, but you can wait to begin the sketches until after your return from up-country."

Elizabeth glared at Jonas and sputtered, "You've got more nerve! What makes you think I'm going to visit your office tomorrow, much less do some artwork for your catalog? Don't you ever give anyone the opportunity to refuse your magnanimous offers?"

Just then the store owner—a short, thin Chinese in a wrinkled white shirt and black trousers—interrupted their discussion. There was a twinkle in his eyes and a smile lit up his face as he greeted them.

"You want?" he asked, indicating the bracelet in Jonas' hand. Obviously he was delighted to have such wealthy-looking foreigners this time of night. But his attitude changed when he heard Jonas begin to bargain in Thai. This wasn't going to be an easy sale, his expression seemed to say.

In spite of being angry, Elizabeth was fascinated at the ensuing exchange. The owner frowned, grimaced and groaned as he reluctantly lowered his price.

"No, no," he kept repeating in English.

Jonas smiled and kindly refused each offer, while adding a little more to the price he would pay. Then he shook his head and put the bracelet back in its place on the counter. It was the signal that the bargaining session was over and the owner said quickly, "OK, OK, you buy." Then giving them a big smile, he took the money Jonas offered and said something to him in Thai which Elizabeth couldn't understand.

It wasn't until she felt the bracelet being slipped on her arm that she realized it was meant for her.

"No," she said, tugging it from her arm as they walked to the front of the small shop. "I don't want anything from you."

"Keep it, Liz."

"No, I don't like being bribed. Get a professional artist to do your work."

"I'm not bribing you and you know it." He took the proffered bracelet and slid it back on her arm, then continued to hold her hand to prevent her pulling it off again. "It's just a pretty little trinket and I thought you might enjoy it. Now, don't be childish."

"I'm not!" she hissed, then looked at him suspiciously. "What did that shopkeeper say to you just now?" The

Chinese had made a wry comment and then looked at Elizabeth with a knowing smile.

"I don't think I'd better tell you. In your present frame of mind, you may get rude." Jonas flipped open the umbrella and helped her off the sidewalk toward the hotel driveway.

Elizabeth threw him a wary glance; she had been unforgiveably rude to him already, as he well knew.

The walk back up the curved driveway was a silent one; Elizabeth was intent on getting her hand released and Jonas was determined she would not succeed. When they reached the hotel, he said, "Sit down a minute, Liz. Please, I want to talk to you."

And she obeyed. Not because she really wanted to, she told herself, but because she was being forced and had no choice but do as he asked. Jonas pulled a chair around to face her and sat back, giving her a thoughtful look.

"Your fiance hurt you deeply, didn't he?"

This surprising question brought a sudden rush of emotions almost impossible to control and she felt the tears filling her eyes and constricting her throat. She looked down at the bracelet and began twisting it around and around her wrist.

Gently, Jonas probed again. "It still hurts, doesn't it?"

Elizabeth clenched her jaws in an effort not to cry. If she once started, the tears she had been holding back since the night the engagement was broken would become an uncontrollable river. She clasped her hands tightly together, trying to suppress the hurt and pain of the open wound within, wanting to be angry with Jonas for forcing her to face the subject once more, but not even able to speak to lash out at him. She just sat there feeling angry and lost and extremely distressed.

"How did he hurt you, Liz?"

The question brought the anger surging above the painful emotions and her answer was like a burst of water from a faucet.

"How? Isn't that rather obvious?"

"Tell me, Liz." He knew he was tearing her apart, but if she didn't talk to someone, get those emotions out in the open, hear her own voice and vindictive words, she might never recover.

"He said he *loved* me," she began angrily. "He said I was the only woman he ever wanted for a wife. He told me so many times that my attributes and gifts complemented his and made him a better man. He said that I was the only one who could make him a complete person; he needed me, he wanted me more than anything else in life. Hah! That's a laugh!" Her voice broke.

"And then?"

"And then," she continued bitterly, "he decided I wasn't as important as the opportunity he was given. He rejected his former desire to serve God overseas, and gave me an ultimatum."

"And when he did that," Jonas added softly, "it seemed to be a total rejection of you as a person. You no longer feel worthwhile, your confidence in any God-given abilities was shattered. You don't trust any man but Martin, do you? You're very bitter."

"I'm not," she protested. "I'm hurt and disappointed. Can't you understand that?"

"Of course. Do you think you're the only person in the world to have a dream crushed?" He paused, then gently made her see the issue. "If you aren't bitter, why is his picture slashed with dark lines? Why do you speak of him with such great hatred in your voice? Why are you so critical of other men? Why . . ."

"Stop it! Stop it!" she whispered, putting trembling hands over her ears to shut out the questions he put before her, questions she had been struggling with ever since that night she had been so easily cast aside.

Jonas reached over and calmly pulled her hands down, and, continuing to hold them, he said, "Liz, you can't afford to let the smallest shred of bitterness stay in your life. It grows more quickly than you can imagine, until it blots out any balanced reasoning in your mind and any communion with God. You've got to . . ."

Elizabeth had had enough. His counsel was correct, but to have a man tell her this rubbed like sandpaper against her bruised mind, and she refused to listen further. Snatching her hands away, she stood up, stopping whatever advice was coming next. And even as she lashed out, she knew she was proving his words true.

"You men are all alike—not one word about *his* unkindness or selfishness! *I'm* the one who needs to change!" Reaching into her skirt pocket for her room key, she said, "I've heard enough. I'm going to bed."

Even then he wouldn't let her alone, but insisted on seeing her to her room. He took the key and inserted it into the door, then kept his hand there so that she might be forced to listen to him.

"Liz, you have too much to offer God, too much happiness ahead of you. Remember that Paul, even while suffering unjustly in prison, wrote that we should relinquish bitterness, and be kind to each other, forgiving just as God has forgiven us."

The smile he gave her then was tender and loving. "Don't be angry with me, Liz." The soft touch of his hand to her face was unsettling. She could fight him for being dictatorial, but not for being gentle.

"Good night, Liz. I'll see you in the morning. By the way, if you'd like to visit the floating markets, I'll pick you up earlier, say about 6:30."

She would agree to any schedule he might suggest for the

next day, if only she could get away from him before she let down her guard. His compassion only triggered her tears. "All right, we'll be ready," she answered quickly. Her good night was just a whisper as she hurriedly moved past him into her room and closed the door.

She took a deep, steadying breath as she stood listening to his footsteps echo down the hallway; then moved forward to see if her brother was still up.

"Martin," she called softly, peeking around the connecting door.

"Martin, Jonas wants to take us to the floating markets tomorrow. We need to be ready by 6:30. Is that agreeable with you?" Her voice was shaking slightly and she cleared her throat, wishing she had never met Jonas Adams.

"That's fine, Liz." Martin looked up from his chair to search her face, wondering what had disturbed her, and saw the pain in her eyes. "Did you have a good time at the shops?" His voice was mild, giving her time to regain her composure.

"What do you think?" she retorted. Turning back to her room, she added, "I'll see you in the morning."

After making preparations for bed, Elizabeth sat down to read the Scriptures. This act was not a childhood habit nor a meaningless ritual which could be ignored if one chose to do so. Even during the times when it was simply a disciplined response, its words were of utmost importance in her life; a vital force and power, a personal message from the God of this universe. Her life would not be complete without it.

Reluctantly, but under compulsion, she turned to the words Jonas had mentioned, for the phrases tumbled about in her mind.

"Forgive one another . . . be tenderhearted . . . put away bitterness."

It was in the fourth chapter of the book of Ephesians,

and she read it over several times, knowing it was not an option in the Christian's life, but a command. Then closing the book, she knelt beside the bed to pray, but that seemed as difficult tonight as the conversation with Jonas had been.

The difficulty lay in her stubbornness to be conformed to God's instructions, not in an inability on His part to hear or to work in a human life. And when she could not feel His presence, it was because she, not God, had moved away.

Finally she slipped under the netting, carefully tucking it under the mattress all the way around the bed, lest any troublesome mosquito find its way in.

At last she reached up to turn off the small bed lamp and smiled, remembering how the netting had made her feel secure as a child; no amount of wild animals of the night could harm her.

If only the wild animals of resentment and bitterness could be as easily dispelled, she thought wearily. Why was it so difficult to recover from this rejection? Resolutely, she pushed such thoughts from her mind and lay listening to the sounds of the Thai night—oriental music composed of full-tone intervals producing tunes strange to the western ear, the strange-sounding siren of an European-made ambulance, someone speaking Chinese in the hallway, and footsteps outside on the veranda.

What she heard next jolted her sleepy mind into full awareness. It was the rattle of metal hitting the protective bars in her window that caused her eyes to fly open in time to see a flashlight beam move slowly around the room.

This wasn't supposed to be part of her first night in Thailand, she thought wildly. What should she do? Bang on the wall for Martin? Sit up and shout at the would-be intruder? Wait to see what would happen next?

Carefully she raised part of the mosquito net so that it wouldn't obstruct her view and saw a long rod coming through the opening to move toward her purse on the table. Someone was trying to rob her!

"Stop it," she shouted, and flung a hand backward to pound on the wall. "Martin, come quick! Thief!"

Martin's feet hit the floor with a *thud* and he came bursting into her room just as she snapped on the wall light. He made a quick grab for the rod and jerked it from unseen hands at the window. They heard voices swearing and the sound of footsteps retreating into the darkness of the night.

Elizabeth sat on the edge of her bed, too stunned to do anything but stare at her brother and feel a great disappointment that this was the final event which capped a bittersweet first day back in Thailand.

"We ought to call the police, or maybe Jonas," Martin said slowly.

"No, I'm sure they won't try again," Elizabeth answered, trying to minimize the incident. "I don't want Jonas around fussing over us and being bossy. I'll just lock my purse in the suitcase and put it in the closet."

"Well, we should at least tell the hotel manager," Martin argued. He walked to the window to look out, not really expecting to see anyone.

"If we do, they'll just call the police. And you know how many robberies there are in the city. Since nothing was taken, the police can't do anything more than keep us up asking questions." Elizabeth dealt efficiently with her purse while she spoke soothingly to him, refusing to put any importance yet to the note she had destroyed at the airport.

"Well . . .," Martin hesitated. His placid nature was leading him to agree.

"If it happens again, we'll call the police, I promise." Elizabeth felt it was an empty concession, for rarely did thieves return, especially if they had been so unsuccessful. "OK," he agreed, turning to check the room. "Is everything put away?''

"Yes. It's all taken care of." She sat down on the bed and began to arrange the netting, wanting to encourage him to go back to bed. "Good night."

"Good night, Liz," he answered hesitantly, and finally clicked off the wall light and went back to his room.

Lying alone in the darkness, Elizabeth found it difficult to be as relaxed as she had pretended. Each little sound from outside her room created new tension, and she held her breath and stared at the window, imagining shadows that weren't there.

Thinking over the day's events, she remembered the re-appearance of the two young people at the hotel desk and wondered if that had anything to do with the attempted robbery. They did look rather shabby and in need of fi-nances. But, no, she shouldn't think ill of them just be-cause they weren't well-dressed.

One of her last thoughts before drifting into a restless sleep was to realize that she had understood the swearing at her window. She and Martin had heard the thwarted burglars speaking in English!

The two young people who were now in Elizabeth's sketchbook were at that moment the center of attention elsewhere. They did not enjoy these meetings, for the man before whom they stood was well-known in the underworld of the city as being one of the most ruthless men in Thai-land—perhaps, even in Southeast Asia.

How they had gotten mixed up with him still rankled in Viv's mind. She glanced bitterly at Phil, and wished she had never asked him along. He was the cause of all this trouble, she thought unreasonably.

They had met in college during her freshman year, had

become friends and then drifted into a serious relationship. Being the stronger-willed of the two, Viv had been the dominant figure in their association. What she wanted, she got. And since Phil was an undemanding, malleable creature, he had responded to her assertiveness and been quite happy to be the follower. Their personalities and needs complemented each other, and for a while, both were content. Then, she decided that rather than stay in college, she would take a trip around the world.

She had heard reports of the easy, exciting life friends had found in other countries. Her spirit was restless, her dreams unfulfilled, and she had thought this trip would be the answer. Her parents had fearfully given her the money she demanded, for they could certainly afford it and they had no other choice, since she had defiantly said that either they give her sufficient funds or they would never see her again.

She did not want to travel alone and knew that Phil would be a good person to take along; he was so pliant, doing whatever she asked, and was more easily managed than anyone else she knew.

Things had gone well for them at first as they worked their way to England on a passenger ship. It was an interesting job, for Viv rather enjoyed cleaning cabins for the officers. After a few weeks in London, she then decided to accept a job offer on a ship sailing around South Africa to Singapore. And, of course, Phil quite willingly agreed to go along.

They sailed around Cape Town, then up to Madagascar, and straight across the Indian Ocean to Ceylon. Just one day's sightseeing in the city of Colombo convinced Viv that she would not care for India, so they went on.

When the ship docked in Singapore, she decided she had had enough of ocean life and they quit their jobs to spend a few enjoyable weeks in that island country. Some of the young people they met were interested in traveling up to Thailand to see the opium fields they had heard so much about, and while Viv wasn't interested in getting involved in the drug scene, she decided that they might as well travel with the group. So, they took a train north through the country of Malaya, up through the long southern tail of Thailand, and, just four months ago, arrived in Bangkok—called the City of Angels by the Thai.

The excitement of being in a new country wore off in two months, and Viv was getting quite tired of Phil. He was homesick, complained all the time, was jealous of her association with anyone else, and was quite dissatisfied when she began spending more time with a group of young people who were involved in political activities.

And then one night it happened. She had been warned to take good care of her passport but had grown careless—perhaps, just to defy Phil's constant mothering. At any rate, she came home to the little shack they shared with two other couples to find that it had been raided—not by the police, but by a band of Chinese, who were known for preying upon the foreigners. All passports were stolen, along with their money and everything else of the slightest value, and the men had been beaten, as a warning not to go to the authorities.

There had been no one around to warn them that they would then be caught in a net of intrigue and crime, that, according to what they now knew, could end in death.

Four weeks ago they had been approached by a man who promised to help them get passports. Viv had been very suspicious, but Phil had, for once, insisted they go. The man led them to Mr. Wong, who had become not a friend, but their master, forcing them deeper and deeper into crime.

Viv had decided she would do whatever was asked, until she could escape—and she had become a hardened young woman, not caring who suffered, as long as it wasn't her. She wasn't about to die in some unknown, impersonal way, like a piece of trash thrown into the river, never to be seen again.

And, as she stood waiting for Mr. Wong to speak, she knew he understood her feelings; he looked at her in amusement and laughed. He only kept her around because he enjoyed tangling with her—she knew that. And while it was a tightrope existence, at least she hadn't been killed, like others he had used.

He spoke, his cultured voice so smooth it aroused fear, his English so pure it was difficult to remember he was Chinese.

"So, you have some information." He played with a small, jewel-studded knife he kept on the desk, and standing up, moved slowly toward her, until the tip of the glistening blade rested on her chin.

"You have found two new prospects?" His voice was low and bland, but she saw the glitter of his eyes.

"Yes," she replied, refusing to lower her eyes from his. "At the airport."

"And where are they now?"

"At the Hotel of the Beautiful Palms."

"And?" The weight of the knife pressed harder against her skin.

"And," she answered, still holding his stare, "Phil and I will have their papers by Monday." She didn't mention they had tried and failed, nor that she intended using those passports before Wong got his hands on them. She hoped it didn't show in her eyes.

When he lowered the knife and turned to look at Phil, she wondered if he had cut the skin but refused to touch her chin while in his presence. She wouldn't allow him that satisfaction.

He grunted, staring at Phil, wondering why he continued

to keep the boy, as he was of absolutely no value—except, perhaps, as a lever with the girl.

Phil shifted uneasily under that stare, and spoke haltingly, trying to hide his fear. "We'll get the passports. We followed them to the hotel and know where their rooms are."

"I hope you do," came the soft reply, "for your sake. You're going to use those passports to leave the country. Would you like that?"

A light of hope flared in Phil's eyes, then died swiftly as he remembered the deceitfulness and cruelty of this man. There was to be nothing good for them in any decision he made, he was sure. Viv had proven useful and Wong would not want to lose her now, not unless she failed him, and she had too much determination to do that. She would be obedient, as long as it was in her best interests. Phil glanced at her and winced inwardly. She was not the same woman who had left the United States; she had grown bitter and hard since becoming involved with Wong, and Phil felt responsible.

Mr. Wong moved back to lean against his desk. He laid the knife down carefully, still looking at it as he talked. "You're going to take some opium out of the country for me and ruin a certain American businessman in the process. I want those passports by Monday morning, no later."

He spoke to Viv, not bothering with Phil, who would die in an opium den up-country when he grew tired of having him around. Viv, he would keep for awhile. At least, he smiled to himself, at least until the end of the week.

"Do you know their names?" he asked Viv.

"No, but they were with Jonas Adams, owner of that import company."

Mr. Wong looked up sharply. "Are you sure?"

"Yes, we saw them having dinner together."

"Very good! That will enrich my plans immeasurably.

By the way, the other American you were working with, John—get him on that opium boat tonight.''

Phil blanched. ''No, he's a good friend, I can't do that to him.''

Mr. Wong frowned and leaned forward. ''Either you get him on that boat, or you will be responsible for killing him,'' he said coolly, showing no concern for the person he had just condemned. ''Take your choice.''

Phil moved forward, his hands clenched at his sides, his anger ready to spill over, but Viv put out a hand to stop him and said, ''We'll take care of it.''

The Chinese laughed at her, amused at her complete disregard for human life. ''I'm sure you will,'' he said, then he motioned to the two guards standing at the doorway.

''Take them away,'' he ordered. He sat down again at his desk and began reading a Chinese newspaper, not bothering to watch the two Americans being led away.

''Monday morning,'' he warned again as they left the room. ''I want those passports.''

Three

The sound of Thai voices in the hallway awakened Elizabeth the next morning, and glancing at her watch, she saw there was little more than an hour's time before Jonas Adams would arrive. Not wanting to add tardiness to the list of sins he seemed to be compiling on her, she hurriedly pulled up the mosquito netting and slipped out of bed.

After a quick shower, she put on a tan blouse—very feminine and cool and trimmed in red—and matching slacks; added a red belt, and slipped on a pair of comfortable sandals. Small red earrings and a tiny gold cross—a gift from her parents which she often wore—finished that part of her preparations. She brushed her hair to a shining bronze, and then added some light make-up to hide the fact that she hadn't slept too well.

There was a hint of the day's heat in the cool air—the reason markets were held in the early morning—and meant that if she wanted to visit any today, it would have to be at the time Jonas had planned. Everything in the room had a slightly damp feeling because of the wet season, but Elizabeth was happy to see that it wasn't raining. Perhaps it would hold off for an hour or two.

Just as she sat down at the desk, Martin looked in to greet her. Seeing that she was about to read, he simply waved and went on with his preparations. She pulled her Bible forward and reached for a special sketch pad she kept just for this time of private communication with God. Along with her Scripture reading, she usually included a sketch for the day: sometimes a prayer request, sometimes a picture of praise, often a word of application which came from her reading. No one ever looked through this book, not even her parents or brother, for they understood its importance in her life and honored her privacy. It was a pictorial commentary of her struggles with life's inequities and corresponding beauty.

She turned to one now—the picture of her former fiance —hoping that soon the words ''Prayer answered'' could be written at the bottom of the page. Well, she might as well admit, sadly, that she wasn't willing yet to release her resentment; she wasn't ready to say that being rejected by one she had loved was all right; she just wasn't ready to forgive that young man. She was too human and not Christ-like enough, she thought, to even pray for blessing in his life.

Jonas' words came to her in quiet warning again: ''It gets lonesome behind those walls you've built.'' She knew that, and she wanted God's best in her life and new work. After all, no one wants wasted years on their account, nor the cutting edge of the Master Gardener's sheers, trimming off withered edges of the soul. Then, why? Why was it so difficult to be rid of the bitterness that kept nipping at her mind?

Sighing, she turned to a new page and stared at its whiteness. What did she most wȧnt to sketch? Unbidden pictures flashed into her mind: Jonas Adams reaching out to befriend her, a Bangkok street scene reminding her of the future, the train which would take them up-country to see her parents.

These were certainly illustrations of present concerns, but what came persistently to her mind's eye, strangely enough, was the two young people she had seen in the airport, imprinted over a picture of a long rod protruding into her hotel room from the window. The thought startled her. Why should she connect those two with the attempted robbery? Perhaps it was because she had heard the robbers speak in English and the two young people kept popping up in her life.

Even while thinking that this idea was more preposterous then predictive, her hand moved quickly to transpose it to paper, and in just a moment, those thoughts were visually before her. Feeling rather puzzled, she put her pen down and turned to read in the third chapter of the book of Psalms.

O Lord, how my adversaries have increased!

The words seemed to jump out at her, but she really thought she had enough of adversaries in the past and hoped it wasn't a prediction of the day's events.

An uneasiness seeped into her mind even as she turned to greet her brother who had just stepped in to suggest a light breakfast in the dining room. "We have just enough time, Liz, for a continental breakfast before Jonas comes."

Afterwards, they took a quick walk along the veranda, stopping just outside their rooms.

"There's nothing here," Martin said, walking slowly over the ground between the hotel and the tall wooden fence. "I was hoping they might have left a clue."

"They did," Elizabeth volunteered.

"What?" Martin looked up sharply. "Where?" He took the steps in two strides, leaping to where Elizabeth stood.

"What did you hear when you jerked that rod through

my window?''

Martin looked at her thoughtfully for a moment. "Well . . . voices and footsteps. Why?" He peered at her over the top of his glasses, which were characteristically slipping down his nose.

"Come on," Elizabeth said, glancing at her watch. "It's almost 6:30. We'd better get around to the front of the hotel before your boss arrives."

"Well?" he urged as they walked together. "What clue?"

She matched her stride to his slower one and asked, "Did you understand what the voices said?"

"Yes, and what foul language," he replied, and then nodded in realization, "Why, it was in English! And if I were a betting person, I'd put my money on the fact that one of those voices was a woman's."

They finished their walk silently while Martin digested this information and Elizabeth wondered if she should tell him about the threatening note and the sketch she had felt compelled to do that morning.

The decision was made for her by the arrival of a small, white European car, driven by Damrong, with Jonas Adams in the front passenger's seat.

"Don't tell Jonas about this, Martin. Please!"

"I don't understand why you're so prickly with him, Liz. He's not out to ruin your life, you know."

She frowned and tossed her head. "I let one man get close to me and look what he did. Jonas Adams can just keep his hands off my life!"

Martin grinned. "Are you sure that's what you want?"

Elizabeth's mouth opened in quick protest, but before she could comment, the man they were discussing stood on the steps before them. And her irritation grew when she turned to greet him—he was wearing a tan sports outfit!

"Good morning," he said·smoothly, smiling at the two of them. "I see we have the same taste in color, Liz. You look very pretty."

Her response was cool, and the two men exchanged amused glances. Martin raised his eyebrows and Jonas just smiled, his look saying that he would handle things quite nicely with Elizabeth, and Martin shouldn't be concerned.

Damrong's greeting was warm and friendly. "Good morning, Miss Thurston, Martin. I hope your first night in our city was a restful one."

Elizabeth flashed Martin a warning look as he moved into the back seat next to her.

"Fine, thank you, Damrong," she answered, not giving her brother an opportunity to respond. *Oh, brother,* she thought, seeing Jonas turn to eye her questioningly, *now what did I do wrong? That man must have antennas for ears.* Her returning look had far more courage in it than she felt, but her eyes challenged him to ask if there was anything wrong.

Then, turning her head, she concentrated on enjoying the sights and sounds of Asian life until they reached a small wooden pier jutting out defiantly into the waters of the Chao Phya River, where Damrong rented a motorboat for them.

Elizabeth allowed Jonas to help her into the boat and she sat down before realizing that Damrong and Martin weren't joining them but getting into a second one instead.

"What are you doing?" she demanded as Jonas eased his long body down beside her.

"Taking you to the floating markets. Why?" He signaled the boatman to proceed and saw her looking at the other boat. "I wanted to give Damrong an opportunity to get to know your brother. Martin is a sharp young man and I think the two of them can develop a deep and lasting friendship."

The complacent look he gave her only increased her suspicion. And then she felt ridiculous. Why should she think this man would ever be romantically interested in her?

And even of more concern, why would she even give that a moment's consideration? He was far more mature and experienced than her former fiance—and was not likely to indulge in romantic interludes simply to amuse himself. She felt her cheeks grow warm in embarrassment when she realized she had been staring at him, and he knew her thoughts. She turned away quickly to look at the buildings that crowded the river's edge like anxious bathers eager to get into the water.

Jonas spoke quietly. "We could have driven to the markets, but this is faster and much more scenic. I thought you'd like a look at Bangkok from this angle." He pointed out several modern tall buildings, shining in the early morning sun and looking out of place among the more common Thai architecture.

"There are so many more hotels now than when you were here last, Liz."

"They aren't nearly as pretty as the temples you can see," she remarked, her hand on the edge of the boat to steady herself, lest she rock even closer to Jonas.

The boat swung around behind a line of barges being pulled into the city from up-country. Jonas smiled and waved at a launch filled with friendly passengers going to work across the river from their homes. Their own boat passed long wooden warehouses, all on stilts, with smaller buildings squeezed in between, reminding Elizabeth of Monopoly houses edging the playing board.

They bounced over the waves left from other boats and turned sharply, causing Elizabeth to lean heavily against Jonas, and he put an arm around her in steadying assistance. Searching her angry face, he said lightly, "I think the boatman is trying to be helpful." His dark eyes sparkled in amusement.

Elizabeth straightened up quickly. "He needn't bother," she said witheringly.

"This isn't the time to argue about it, but you and I, Elizabeth Thurston, are going to have a long talk today."

"Is that a warning?" she asked, watching the boat slow down and move cautiously into a canal crowded with long, narrow boats. "It may be a one-sided conversation; I have nothing to discuss with you."

"It may be one-sided, all right," he replied, smiling at her irritation.

Their boatman said something to Jonas and he nodded. The boat was pulled expertly up to a pier and tied there; just then the floating market was before them.

"Wonderful, just wonderful!" she whispered, and in the excitement of watching a scene she had witnessed many times as a child, forgot to keep her guard up. Her eyes danced and the delighted smile she gave Jonas brought him much satisfaction. This was the woman he was interested in; he knew there was much more warmth and tenderness and caring under the protective shell she had erected. He was prepared to spend the time necessary to bring her back to life again. She was a child of God and meant for higher and better things than what she was experiencing now. Those who allowed bitterness to fester in their lives would, sooner or later, be completely ruled by that emotion. Every thought, every decision, and every attempted enjoyment was experienced in relationship to the resentment, until every waking moment was under its authority.

"There must be two dozen skiffs right here," she whispered. Her eyes darted from boat to boat and she named the items that filled the baskets.

"Eggplant, Chinese cabbage, cucumbers, custard apples, mangostines, bananas, bottles of fish sauce, summer onions and ginger root."

Another boat slid slowly past them and Elizabeth counted

the baskets. "There are ten in that one, and each has a different vegetable."

Her hand drew delicate lines over the white paper that was braced on her lap to prevent any slip of the pen in the movement of the water. She drew the skiff they had just seen, ladened with vegetables and maneuvered by a Thai woman in a colorfully printed blouse and orange sarong. A wide-brimmed hat, shaped like a lampshade, lay on the basket in front of her. The man seated in the other end of the boat was dealing with a customer whose crouched position on the pier would have been most uncomfortable to a foreigner.

Elizabeth was so engrossed with her drawings that she wasn't aware of the passing of time, nor of the man who sat so contented and quiet at her side. It seemed as though she had just gotten started when he spoke.

"Well done, Liz." He glanced at his watch. "Do you know how long you've been at that?"

"No," she murmured, not wanting to break the spell sketching always had on her. "We haven't been here long, have we?"

He chuckled softly. "Just about an hour."

Her hand was arrested. "Not that long, surely!" She was dismayed at having detained him. "Why didn't you tell me? I've kept you from your work." It was difficult to apologize, for she still wanted to take her resentment out on him, but she knew he had acted out of kindness. "I . . . I'm sorry," she admitted hesitantly. "I get so carried away." She closed the pad abruptly and jammed the pen into her purse.

"Don't apologize, Liz. I haven't enjoyed anything like this for a long time. You've given me a new look at something I've taken for granted, and I've had as pleasant a time as you. And besides," he added kindly, "I've not seen you so relaxed and happy. It needs to happen more often."

Elizabeth flipped through the pages she had done, unable to meet his look and replied stiffly, "I'm ready to go whenever you are."

The crowded canal had thinned out considerably and Elizabeth turned to see the boat carrying Martin and Damrong glide silently toward them. Martin called out as they passed by, "Do any pictures, Liz?"

"A few," she answered diffidently, still feeling chagrined for having kept Jonas too long.

He turned and spoke to their boatman. The motor came to life, the rope was untied, and they prepared to follow the others down the canal and back into the Chao Phya River.

Elizabeth watched the man guiding Martin's boat. He's Chinese, she thought, and probably in his thirties, taller than most, with a muscular build that hinted at an ability in the martial arts. And there was something unusual about him, though she couldn't define it for a few minutes.

She continued to study him, watching as he started the motor and then guided the boat down the canal. As they got closer, she observed his movements, and then it came to her. He looked too well-fed to be a typical boatman, too clean, and even too elegant in spite of his tattered clothes. He seemed out-of-place. She wanted to be sure to get a good look at his face when they docked across the river, so she could sketch him. That extra sense, an artist's eye to see the minute things others did not notice, and the schooling to distinguish shades of color, distances, textures and even feelings, made her positive about her judgment and intrigued about the reason for this enigma.

The two boats surged into the river, moving in and out of traffic with ease, and Elizabeth watched idly, almost mesmerized by the motion of the boat against the water.

Two things happened almost simultaneously. First, it began to rain—a hard, driving rain that had the two of them drenched before Jonas could open an umbrella. And while they were both intent upon getting immediate shelter, their boatman yelled a warning and pulled the boat sharply to the left.

"What in the world!" Jonas exclaimed, dropping the umbrella and throwing an arm around Elizabeth to pull her tightly to him. "Hang on," he ordered. And for once, she was happy to obey.

The boat tipped as a wave washed over the side; they leaned away, trying to help right the craft and heard another engine, louder and stronger than theirs, churning up the water close by.

Their boatman gunned the motor and pulled sharply away, bringing the craft under control as he did so. He was shouting and shaking an angry fist at the offending boater.

Jonas released Elizabeth and turned to look back; he couldn't see any identifying marks on the other boat and was frustrated that it turned and sped down river away from them.

"Who was it?" he asked their boatman.

The man shook his head, and replied heatedly that he had no idea, but that he wished the gods of the river would swallow the other boat whole, and right on the spot!

"Probably some young kid racing a boat like American kids race cars," Jonas said to Elizabeth. "Are you all right?" He reached down to retrieve the umbrella, but the rain stopped and the sun came out.

"I'm fine. Or, at least I will be when I dry off a bit." She looked with dismay at her sketch pad. It had slid to the floor in the excitement and was a soggy mess. She picked it up and let the water drip off the pages. "Well, I can redo the pictures. Better that than being overturned in the middle of the river."

When they got to the pier they were met by a concerned Martin who had to be assured several times that they were not hurt. He helped Elizabeth from the boat and then handed her a sweater he had gotten from the car. "Are you cold?"

"A little," she confessed, happy to slip the sweater over her shoulders. She turned to see Jonas paying the boatman, and then remembered the man in Martin's boat.

He was still there, and having an earnest conversation with Damrong who handed him some Thai bills and stepped out of the boat. Then, when the man called Damrong back for more words, she saw his face, and it only deepened her instinct that he was an unusual boatman. He looked far too intelligent for such work, and his attitude toward Damrong was one of authority. He spoke in a low voice, frowning and emphasizing his sentence with a quick nod of the head. Then he sat down, switched on the motor, and pulled out into the river.

"Damrong," Elizabeth asked curiously as he joined them on the pier. "Do you know that man very well?"

Damrong's smile was congenial but his voice sounded uneasy. "No, I see him sometimes on the river." A shrug of the shoulders punctuated his reply. Then he turned quickly and moved toward the car, almost as though he did not wish to prolong their conversation.

Elizabeth shook herself mentally as she walked up the pier with Martin. There must be something exotic in the Bangkok air that made her overly sensitive. She took the towel Jonas offered and began to wipe the rain from her face and arms.

"Damrong, why don't you take a taxi back to the office," Jonas said. "I'll swing by the hotel so Martin and Elizabeth can change clothes before we do anything else."

"OK," Damrong replied. He seemed willing, almost relieved to do as his employer had asked; he shot a quick glance at the others and said, "I'll see you later."

The remainder of the morning was spent visiting the other places Elizabeth had wanted to see that day. They stopped by the radio station in order to leave the long-awaited tapes of Thai hymns, and then drove to the house where she and Martin had once lived as children.

They stopped for a few minutes at the Phra Mane Grounds, a large field in front of the Grand Palace where weekend markets were held.

"It's always a colorful place," Martin said, as they sat in the car watching the people strolling and bargaining and eating. "Looks like a holiday carnival."

There were uniformed men from the armed services in search of a good buy; other men wore the usual business attire—a white shirt and dark trousers. There were women in brightly-colored, long sarong skirts. and others in western skirts and blouses.

"If we took time now to investigate all those stalls, I expect we'd find almost anything you might want, with the exception of large appliances," Jonas informed them, and Elizabeth agreed.

She was about to ask Martin if they had time to visit just one or two of the make-shift shops when she caught sight of the same two people that were becoming a growing puzzle for her. They were standing under the shade of a nearby tree and arguing in low, restrained voices. As she watched, the girl glanced up and saw Elizabeth staring at her. She spoke hurriedly to the man with her, grabbed his arm and pushed him behind a stall and out of sight. Elizabeth felt a shiver go through her, so strong was the impression that she and Martin were going to have some kind of confrontation with those two.

"Elizabeth," Martin said, looking at her from the front seat of the car, "are you cold?"

"N...no," she answered. "I'm fine."

"I thought I saw you shiver."

"It's nothing," she replied, smiling brightly at him. "Let's come back here after we've been up-country, Martin. I'd like to buy a few things to send to some of my college friends." She looked up to see Jonas watching her through the rear-view mirror, and perversely, it sealed her determination not to tell him what she had just seen.

"Are you ready for lunch?" he asked, still watching her closely.

Elizabeth was ready, in fact, she was famished, but stubbornly answered him indifferently, "Whenever you wish."

"We can have lunch at a special little Chinese place I know, and we'll drive by my place on the way."

His house was in one section of the city where most of the residences were modern and extremely expensive-looking. His was a true Thai home—built of polished wood and sitting on stilts, with large shutters that would open to the breezes. And in its simplicity, it seemed far more elegant than the ultra-modern, Western architecture of the neighboring houses.

The grounds around it were well-kept and profuse with frangipani and bougainvillaea shrubs. A veranda ran full-length across the front and there were hanging pots filled with bright flowers and luxuriant ferns. It was the prettiest house in the entire section. She wanted to stay for a tour of its interior, but, obdurately, would rather bite off her tongue than ask.

She felt a compulsive need to dislike this man, and as they drove away she began working on that again. She reviewed all the hurt she had endured recently, and then transferred that pain to Jonas Adams' account, staring at the back of his head and thinking of all the mean, despicable things men did to women. She wouldn't trust one ever again, except Martin and her father, she thought parenthetically.

All during lunch at the restaurant, she worked on this project, again lapsing into long silences while Martin and Jonas talked, and searching the room for anything that would take her mind away from the genuine kindness she felt in Jonas Adams. She was even grateful for the diversion of the military police coming in to check passports.

By the time lunch was over and they were on their way to his office, Elizabeth underscored one item on her list: Jonas was assuredly the most dictatorial man she had ever met. He had comandeered their day, with Martin agreeing to his every suggestion. It made no difference, thought Elizabeth, that he was doing all the things she had been dreaming of for months—he was just bossy!

Well, he had mentioned at lunch that he was flying to India that night, so she could put up with his autocratic methods for one day if she knew he wouldn't be around for a few weeks. Now he wanted them to tour his export business before returning to the hotel. And when they arrived at *Adams Export, Ltd.* , she was secretly glad they had come.

The building was one of the most beautiful she had seen. It wasn't much larger than any others on the block, but it out-classed them all as far as she was concerned. It was entirely fronted with glass which jutted out at evenly spaced intervals in floor-to-ceiling diamond shapes. In each of these areas, she saw some of his merchandise dramatically displayed; it was impossible not to want every item in the window.

Inside, she met Adams' secretary, a pretty Chinese girl named Joy, who seemed eager to befriend Elizabeth and to peek as often as she could at Martin.

When Jonas asked Elizabeth to accompany him to his office in order to look at his new catalog ideas, she heard Joy ask Martin if he would like a tour, and saw her brother respond graciously and, perhaps, even a bit eagerly.

"What are you smiling at?" Jonas asked as he led her up a short, spiral staircase to his office, which overlooked the main floor.

"Your secretary . . . is she married?"

"No, why do you ask?"

"She seems interested in Martin," Elizabeth answered as she stood at the large picture window, looking down upon the couple as they moved slowly about the display room.

Jonas grunted softly and moved away from Elizabeth. "Well, she's a great secretary. I don't want to lose her, not even to Martin." He bent over the catalog spread out on his desk. "Here's what I want you to see, Liz."

Elizabeth waited for him to ask her to come and look at the material, but he was silent, his mind already filled with ideas. She sighed and gave in, walking toward him slowly. "Don't you ever ask politely?"

He looked up in surprise. Then, realizing what she meant, smiled broadly and said softly, "Please," and pulled out a leather desk chair for her to use.

After they had gone over every page, with Jonas telling her briefly what he wanted, Elizabeth saw that his idea had merit, but was still determined not to get involved. She wanted nothing to do with Jonas Adams. She was in Bangkok to devote her time to the radio ministry.

"Will you do a couple of sketches for me, Liz?" Still leaning over the desk, he closed the catalog and turned to watch for her answer. His face was too close to hers and she sat back abruptly in the chair.

"No."

"Just a couple that I can use when I show this to my board members."

"No! I don't want to get involved. I'm going to be too busy."

"I mean right now, today. It won't take you long." He took her by the hand and pulled her up to stand beside him. Then he grinned down at her reluctant expression. "Please," he pleaded softly. "Just two."

"All right! Just two. Then will you leave me alone?"

"Great!" He walked quickly toward the office door, her hand still in his. "We'll have to go to the supply room downstairs."

They started down the staircase and Elizabeth sighed with relief when he released her hand. She certainly didn't want anyone getting the wrong impression about their relationship. He was much too dictatorial for her. She would do the sketches just to be left alone!

Jonas led her to a long desk on the right wall of the supply room, put paper and several pens in front of her, and then moved to the shelves to choose two items for her to sketch. One was an exquisite black-lacquered bowl with lotus buds painted in the finish. The other was a small, perfectly-shaped sugar spoon made of bronze with black wood inlaid on the handle. He placed the two items on the desk in front of her just as Joy opened the door and peered in.

"Jonas," she called softly, her accent lilting and dainty, "there is a telephone call for you from Hong Kong."

He excused himself and left the room, and for a full half-hour Elizabeth was alone with her artwork, getting caught up again in the magic of pen and paper. No matter how much time she spent in this craft, she never grew tired of it. And she was beginning to suspect that Jonas knew that and had tempted her with "just two sketches," thinking she could never bring herself to do less than the best. The finished product would be a good one and, perhaps, she would be eager to complete the catalog.

She inspected the two sketches on the desk, and satisfied with what she saw, penned her initials in the corner.

As she sat back to enjoy the quietness, she suddenly heard voices arguing at the back of the room, and turning, recognized Damrong, who was obviously displeased with his companion. When he turned to see her watching, he spoke sharply to the other man, who nodded quickly, and left by the back door.

Damrong moved toward her, smiling slightly, his manner typically polite, but this time she felt it was assumed.

"Having trouble?" she asked.

"Well, you know how it can be sometimes; people not fulfilling their responsibilities." He glanced back at the closed door, then turned again. "Are you working for us now?"

"Just some sketches Jonas wanted," she said, waving toward the desk.

Before she could think of any more questions to ask about the argument, the inner door opened and Jonas came striding in. And just as other times when he came near her, Elizabeth felt as though an electrical charge had been sent through the room. She wondered if other people felt his vibrant nature as she did.

She waited silently as he moved to her side and looked down at her work. She knew it was good, not with undue pride, but with a sense of experience and knowledge of her abilities.

Damrong still seemed caught in the unpleasant scene she had witnessed, and he asked in a low voice, "Did I bother you just now? I did not know you were in the room, and I had a problem with . . . a delivery man."

Elizabeth was sure he did not wish Jonas to hear the question. She could hardly catch his words. But whether Damrong was being considerate of Jonas' concentration on her artwork, or whether there was something suspicious going on, she could not decide.

"There wasn't any problem, Damrong," she answered quietly, her sober eyes questioning his. "I had finished my work."

"Terrific!" Jonas was pleased. "Just what I wanted. Damrong, look at what she's done for us."

Damrong turned troubled eyes from Elizabeth and glanced at the pictures Jonas had in his hands. "You have great talent, Miss Thurston. They look quite real." His voice was not quite sincere, his glance but a brief one. And, then to add to Elizabeth's puzzlement, he glanced at the boxes from which the pieces had been taken, looked back at the empty places on the shelves, and then frowned at Jonas. Elizabeth wondered what he was thinking, but Jonas cut off her question when he picked up the small sugar spoon and put it in her hand.

"Here," he said, "I'd like you to have this—for your work today."

Elizabeth shook her head. "No, I don't need any pay."

"Take it," Jonas argued. "It's just a piece of bronze work. It isn't that expensive."

She gave in, deciding once more that it was easier to comply with his wish than to resist. She looked at Damrong again, his strange behavior on her mind.

What she saw wasn't what she had expected. He took a close look at the spoon and frowned, opened his mouth to make a comment, then closed it without a word. His glance at Jonas was still a worried one before his face became inscrutable. Jonas was inspecting the two sketches again and missed all of this, but Elizabeth hadn't, and she felt uneasy.

"Is there something wrong, Damrong?"

"No," he replied quickly. "I . . . I only thought I saw a flaw on the spoon, but I was mistaken." He moved away from the desk and spoke to Jonas. "If you don't mind" a slight accent slurring his speech increased Elizabeth's feeling that he was agitated, and he continued, "I will work on the new accounts now." He watched her slip the spoon into her shoulder purse, and then excused himself.

"Damrong," Jonas called, "would you take these sketches to my office, please. I don't want them ruined."

Damrong reached for the papers and with one more strange glance at Elizabeth, turned and left the room.

"Come on, Liz," Jonas said as he ushered her to the door, "Let's see if Martin is ready to return to the hotel. You've had quite a morning and you ought to have a rest." He glanced down for her reaction and smiled at her frown. "Martin and Damrong are going to see a Thai boxing match tonight. I'd like to take you to dinner, if you'll come."

"Do I have a choice?" she asked with resignation.

"No," he replied with the smile that was becoming more of a pleasure to watch than she cared to admit.

A short while later, Jonas dropped them off at their hotel, telling Elizabeth that he would meet her there at six o'clock that evening. Martin stopped at the hotel desk to buy a newspaper and Elizabeth went on to her room.

She opened the door and stood transfixed. There, taped on the wall mirror, was a large piece of paper with five words printed in bold black letters.

"WE WON'T MISS NEXT TIME!"

She glanced quickly about the room, fearing someone might be waiting; and stepping inside, she closed the door with shaking hands and leaned back against its sturdiness, staring in disbelief at the ugly message. Who was doing this? What on earth did they want?

Never before had she felt such empathy for the Psalm writer whose words she had just read that morning: "Oh, Lord, how my adversaries have increased!"

Suddenly she was furious. Who would dare do such a thing! Obviously, some prankster with a perverted sense of humor, and not worth the worry. She marched over to the mirror, ripped off the offending message, and started to tear it into shreds. Then she changed her mind. Perhaps she should keep it, just in case. Angrily, she folded the paper and thrust it into the back of her sketch book. Then she opened the desk drawer and put the bronze spoon in the box with the silver bracelet Jonas had given her.

Suddenly realizing how drained she felt, she sank down wearily on the edge of her bed. It was probably a reaction to all the excitement. A good nap would put her back in balance and then she could make some sense of all these strange events. She heard Martin enter his room, whistling under his breath, and smiled. That brother was one of the sanest things she had in her life now, and she was grateful. Lying back on the bed, she determinedly put aside thoughts about threatening notes and boat mishaps and closed her eyes.

Two hours later she awoke with a start to hear Martin tapping lightly on her door, and was surprised that she had slept so soundly. The note, still hidden yet in her sketch book, came quickly to mind. She could still see it on the mirror, and realized that it had fulfilled its purpose—she was uneasy and concerned. Perhaps she should tell Martin, but that could be decided while she was getting ready. A shower would wash away the sluggishness after such a long nap, and she could look at things in proper perspective.

She noted with irritation that the message was still having its effect—she looked nervously down the hallway on her way to and from the shower and locked her door after returning. It was comforting to know Martin was nearby.

The reason she chose to wear her favorite dress—a pale blue silk with long, full sleeves—was not to impress Jonas, she told herself sternly, but because he was taking her to a restaurant on the top floor of one of those opulent hotels she had seen earlier. The dress was a shade that brought out the blue of her eyes and added a rich hue to her hair. It was complimentary and bolstered her confidence as she suddenly remembered Jonas' threat to have a long talk. Well, she wasn't going to hide from him, nor allow him to be a tyrant in her life. She could take care of herself, and she would be sure to let him know exactly that if necessary.

But when he arrived at her door a short while later, she took a deep breath before responding to his knock, feeling as though she were about to take the witness stand in her own behalf.

"You look beautiful," he said appreciatively, holding out a small white orchid. "From my own garden. Will you wear it?"

She nodded, silently taking the flower to pin on her dress. Then she turned toward him. "I've never had an orchid before, thank you."

"In that case," he replied, taking her hand to pull her closer, "I'll see that you have one every day." He stood looking down at her, not speaking, but just taking a close inventory of her face, the expression in her eyes, and lipstick she wore. She pulled away, frightened of that intent look. "Are you hungry, Liz?" Seeing her nod, he added, "Then, let's go."

When they were seated at a table by the window overlooking the river, Elizabeth was delighted with the view. She could enjoy the lights of the city while Jonas ordered a seafood dinner. Finally he sat back in his chair, that one lock of hair falling over his forehead, and looked across the table at her. "Have you had a good day?"

"Yes," she replied, but a shadow crossed her eyes as

she thought of the sinister events that seemed to be inexorably piling up—the note at the airport, the attempted robbery, a near mishap in the river, Damrong's strange reactions, and the note on her mirror.

"What's the matter?" He saw her reaction immediately. "You're not worried about the boat incident, are you? Don't be, for I've already asked Damrong to investigate it for me."

"I'm just a bit travel-weary, I suppose," she said, wondering silently if Damrong already knew the reason for the near accident. He had talked for a long time with a boatman he only saw occasionally on the river.

She waited nervously all through the delicious meal, through the Thai dance exhibition and the performance of a Thai orchestra . . . but the promised long talk did not come. Perhaps Jonas had forgotten his threat and she was setting up her defenses for nothing. Finally, she relaxed completely and began to talk easily about her art interests, her future career, and even shared some of her experiences as a child in this country she loved.

Jonas never took his dark eyes from her face while they talked, and skillfully asked questions that drew all this information from her. She glanced up once to see a woman at the next table eyeing him enviously, and had to admit that he was attractive. But, she thought, looks don't mean a thing! He was, however, attentive and gentle—that she had to admit—and her face grew animated and her eyes a deeper blue as she hesitantly answered his inquiry about her life goals.

He shared with her as well—of his childhood days in a small town in Illinois where a desire to work overseas became a life goal, of his formal education, and of his commitment to serving God through his vocational abilities. He had met a Christian businessman in New York who encouraged him to become a junior partner until his goal of establishing a business in Thailand was finally reached.

As she listened, Elizabeth conceeded unwillingly that only a man of his drive and dedication could accomplish what he had done. And, only someone with such courage could determine to set up a stronghold of Christian testimony in the business world, and then demonstrate a moral responsibility to the social needs of the community. He wasn't taking any praise for himself, either.

"God has guided and given wisdom, and opened many hearts to His love through it all. It's His business, you know."

They fell silent, thinking of God's work in their lives. Elizabeth found herself comparing Jonas with her former fiance; she was forced to admit to the tiny misgivings she had felt with Peter. He had never really had the kind of character she could trust and admire. She could see that now and it reflected upon her ability to make choices. And it still didn't lessen the hurt she felt. Staring out the window into the darkness of the night, she shivered and her grasp of an unused spoon on the table tightened.

Jonas saw the pain in her eyes and his hand reached out to cover hers. "Don't," he whispered. "Don't put yourself through that pain any more."

His hand still on hers, he signaled for the waiter and paid the bill. Then he stood up, helped her to her feet, and silently they moved around the scattered tables—most now empty—and out into the lobby.

Expecting him to walk toward the elevators, Elizabeth was surprised when he turned to one of the small rooms off the large hallway, pushed open the door and led her inside. There were several chairs, a lounge, and a small writing desk. Her feet sank into the rich thickness of the green rug, and she felt the intimate atmosphere of the stylish sitting room.

Jonas led her to a high-backed chair facing a window

and sat down on the window seat in front of her, still holding her hand and watching her closely.

"Could we go home?" Elizabeth's voice was low and a little shaky, and she stared ahead, refusing to return his look.

"Home?" he asked gently, a world of meaning in his question.

"To the hotel," she amended. "I . . . I'm tired."

"But don't you want to see the view from here? Look, there are the lights of the Grand Palace." He turned and pointed out the window. "It's funny how distance changes your perspective."

Elizabeth turned to look at him then, wariness growing in her expression. "Is that an introduction to this long talk we're to have?"

Deep inside she had known all along she was not going to escape, so it was just as well to mention the subject herself. She tried to take her hand from his, but his grip only tightened.

"What is his name?" he asked, startling her so much that her hand jerked in his. "Your ex-fia . . ."

"I know who you mean! My former fiance's name," she said slowly and distinctly, "is Peter. Peter Allen."

"Your voice is filled with loathing, did you know that?" He wasn't making an accusation, merely a statement. It was his intention to help her work through her bitterness, not beat her to death with it.

She closed her eyes and leaned back against the chair in resignation. She felt Jonas touch a curl on the side of her face, and turned away.

His voice was gentle. "Do you know the high cost of allowing such feelings to grow in your life?"

"Of course, I know," she replied, raising her head to frown at him. "It can destroy you—physically and spiritually."

"Then, why? Don't you care?"

"Yes, I care!"

"Then do something about it," he challenged softly.

"But you just don't understand!" Her hand hit the arm of the chair in protest. "Men, especially one like you, never allow themselves to be placed in a position where they can be hurt."

"Do you think," he asked, leaning closer, "that I've never been hurt?"

He waited for her response, and when there was none, continued.

"Anyone who opens himself up to love, always opens himself up to pain and suffering. Love makes you vulnerable. It made Christ so vulnerable that He died for us."

He shifted on the window seat so that he might see her face better. "Liz, you aren't any different from millions of others who have felt pain, for one reason or another. Of course I admit that a discarded and trampled-on love causes injury! But, I've heard it said that troubles for the strong only make them stronger; but for the weak, only weaker."

"And you've decided I'm weak." Her voice was angry in self-defense.

"No, I'm saying you can either go down in defeat and live a miserable, miserly, lonely life, or . . . or else you can give up your right to revengeful feelings and be thankful for this."

"Thankful! That's asking a lot, isn't it?"

"It's the only way, Liz. I've met some extremely bitter people. They believe everyone is against them, imposing ulterior motives on every action and word, until no one wants to be around them. They don't trust others and refuse all offers of friendship. Then, they feel completely unloved and can't understand why. In an effort to feel worthwhile, they magnify the mistakes and imperfections of others. They build walls which they think are protective, but are, in reality, prisons of loneliness and misery. I don't want to see you like that. For your own sake, you must forgive him."

Elizabeth jerked her hand from his and said vindictively, "He doesn't deserve forgiveness!"

"Do you?"

"Wh-what? What do you mean? I didn't treat him like dirt!"

"I mean that none of us are worthy of God's forgiveness, but we have it anyway."

Elizabeth heard people talking in the lobby, and their laughter rang out like a mockery of her wounds.

"You told me earlier this evening that you wanted to work for God in Thailand. Your face was alive with a desire to please Him. But you can't be of help to the work of God if you aren't willing to change. And, your will is important—you decide whether you will continue to hate, to the point of physical illness, or whether you will forgive. It's a matter of choice. I know that grieving the Spirit of God is not what you really want to do, but you are."

He pulled a small New Testament from his pocket and turned to the words in Ephesians he had mentioned the night before. "Look," he said gently, pointing to the verse. "What does it say?"

Elizabeth stared at the page, unwilling to answer, but the words burned in her mind as he repeated them slowly.

"Do not grieve the Holy Spirit of God . . . let all bitterness and wrath and anger and clamor and slander be put away from you, along with malice."

A tear slipped from her eye and started to fall slowly down her cheek. She sat with clenched hands, wanting to strike out at this man who was making her face the truth again. She felt his finger touch the tear and wipe it away, but he went on, relentlessly, kindly, to deal with her problem.

"And the next verse says, 'Be kind to one another, tenderhearted, forgiving . . .'" he paused for emphasis, "' . . . forgiving each other, just as God in Christ has forgiven you.'"

There was a long silence in the room as Elizabeth sat fighting everything she had just heard. It wasn't that she did not know it was true, but something perverse and obstinate made her stubbornly refuse to give in, and her tears dried up. She would not admit her wrong in front of Jonas Adams! She would not forgive Peter Allen! She just couldn't. She did not know whether she wanted to scream or slap this man who was humiliating her so. He had no right!

She pushed back her chair and stood up, shaking all over from her distress and anger. She would not stand for this another minute! She would take a taxi back to the hotel if necessary, but she would not listen to him any more!

He unfolded his long body from the window seat and stood up, his hands on her arms to prevent her running from the room, and he could feel her trembling.

"Oh, Liz," he said tenderly, "if you only knew how I . . ." He stopped, wisely refraining from finishing the sentence. He had so much he wanted to share with this lovely young woman who had come bursting into his life, but it would have to wait. She had to deal with her bitterness first. He smiled down into her unhappy face and pulled her closer, holding her in his arms as a brother would hold a sorrowing sister, until finally the trembling stopped and he heard her muffled voice against his coat.

"You're going to ruin my orchid."

He looked down at her and asked seriously. "Does it matter to you?"

"Yes. It's the first one I've ever had."

Then she turned abruptly to leave the room, and he followed her to the elevators.

They did not talk much as he drove back to her hotel; he

had counseled without her consent and said more than enough for one night. He would just rest in the fact that God would bring healing.

She felt him glance at her several times, but refused to respond, and when he tried to take her hand, she pulled away, moving closer to the door.

"Can't I hold your hand?" he asked quizzically.

"What for?" she retorted.

"Elizabeth," he warned and held out his hand. It was a battle of wills, and she refused to give in.

When they stopped at the next intersection, he turned to her and said quietly, "Please. I don't want you angry with me."

"Hm! You can hold my hand, but I will still be angry . . ." She stopped, knowing that while she was directing her anger at Jonas and Peter, she really was blaming God, and that wasn't what she wanted at all! If she believed that He ruled every circumstance of life, and if He in His wisdom made no mistakes, then she ought to believe it was all for the best. But could you experience God's best and still be unhappy?

She turned to see how he was taking her outbursts of anger and saw him glance several times into the rear-view mirror with a preoccupied expression. Looking over her shoulder, she asked, "What's the matter? Is someone following us?"

"I doubt it," he replied smoothly.

But she wasn't to be put off; this would be the perfect ending for the emotional roller-coaster she had been on all day, she thought cynically as she turned around in her seat and watched. For several blocks a black car followed theirs, moving into each lane Jonas chose, turning at each corner as they did, making no attempt to conceal their pursuit.

"What are you going to do?"

"Nothing," he replied, smiling at her. "If they want something of me, I'll know sooner or later." And with that, he pulled into the long, curving driveway of the hotel and stopped near the entrance. The black car moved on down the street and out of sight. He cut the motor and turned to look at her.

"Have I been too hard on you tonight?" he asked, finally reaching over for her hand. "I wouldn't talk to you like this, Liz, if I didn't care. Please believe that." He saw from her expression that she didn't, that she was full of distrust. "I'm leaving Bangkok just as soon as I get to the airport tonight, and when I return at the end of the week, you'll be in Chiangmai for two weeks. I don't want hard feelings between us for that long."

He was wanting the kind of concession from Elizabeth that she refused to give. "I've had all the turmoil I can take for one day, Jonas Adams," she cried, and turning, wrenched open her door and hurriedly got out of the car.

Jonas caught up with her at the steps of the veranda. "Liz," he said, putting out a hand to stop her flight. "Liz, wait."

He pulled her into his arms and looked down into her face, searching her eyes for the response he wanted. "I don't want you unhappy. Don't you realize what you mean to me?"

Elizabeth felt his strength—that solid strength she could depend on; if only she did not have visions of him treating her as Peter had. The concern and gentleness she saw in Jonas had never been part of Peter's nature, but it was Jonas' strength that frightened her. If she ever gave in to trust him completely, she would be lost. His rejection would be far more powerful and lasting than Peter Allen's could ever be. She would never recover from the havoc this man could wreak in her life. No, men were all alike; she had been hurt once, that was enough!

"Liz, you are very beautiful," he whispered, his eyes searching her face in the dim veranda light and bringing a wave of fear surging through her like a flood, any rational thoughts she might have had vanished.

"Let me go," she cried out softly, and turning, she ran up the steps and into the hotel—away from the dangerous relationship his presence implied.

Jonas stood watching her disappear, the evening ending on a note he did not like, then turned and walked slowly back to his car. He glanced at his watch—he did not have time to try reasoning with her. In fact, he barely had enough time to get to the airport to meet his pilot for their scheduled flight to India, and he would also need to call Damrong about that black car now moving slowly down the street from the hotel.

On the way to the airport, he prayed for Elizabeth, committing everything to God, knowing that only He can change hearts and rebuild lives.

He did not know how desperately Elizabeth was going to need that prayer, for she was to discover when she reached her hotel room, that she was not finished with the emotional upheavals of the day—not for a long time!

Four

Elizabeth was boiling over with conflicting emotions when she left Jonas standing by the veranda steps to storm back to her room. She felt angry with him, overcome with shame and guilt, and saddened to realize she deserved his admonitions. All of this, on top of a growing apprehension over warnings and spying strangers and thieves, made her feel physically ill. Her head was pounding by the time she approached her room; all she wanted to do now was take some aspirin and go straight to bed.

But that wish was not to be fulfilled.

What she saw when she opened the door and flicked on the light shocked her into numb disbelief. She began to tremble, and a cold fear spread through her body as she stepped in and silently closed the door.

The bed was torn apart, clothes were thrown everywhere, suitcases lay open with their contents spilling out, everything from the desk lay tossed on the floor. The room was in total chaos.

Someone had searched—meticulously and thoroughly—

through everything, and with vindictive pleasure had left things in as much disarray as possible.

Elizabeth put a shaky hand to her forehead, pressing hard to stop the pain. She didn't know how much more strain she could take. If only she had allowed Jonas to accompany her to her room. At least, she wouldn't be standing here alone and frightened, wondering if someone was waiting in Martin's room, waiting to do her physical harm. She stood rooted to the spot as she fought an overwhelming urge to turn and run.

But, she couldn't. Where would she go? Jonas was on his way to the airport and she had no idea where to find Martin. Besides, she had to know if there was someone in his room. Cautiously, she inched toward the connecting door. It stood slightly ajar, and she pushed it open slowly and peered in.

The condition of his room was a copy of hers—except that, on the floor, laying face-down amid the jumble of upturned furniture and clothing, was her brother!

"Martin!" she cried, rushing to kneel beside him. Frantically, she felt his wrist for a pulse and touched his face for reassurance that he was alive. "What happened? Martin, speak to me!"

He groaned and painfully turned over on his back. His face was swollen and there was a cut on his chin. With great relief that he could respond, she said, "Lie still for a minute."

But he struggled to sit up, moving very carefully and moaning in pain.

"Where do you hurt?" She put a supporting arm around his shoulders to steady his movement.

"My head," he whispered, his lips barely moving.

"Perhaps you'd better not move. Should I call a doctor?"

"No, don't! I'll be fine, Liz. Just give me a minute or two."

She helped him stand and move to the only chair that hadn't been upset. Then, picking up one beside him, she sat down and took his hand. "Who . . . who did this?" she asked—somehow already knowing the answer.

"Would you believe," he spoke with difficulty. "Would you believe those two young people you sketched?" Martin rubbed the back of his neck and then asked if she could find his glasses. "They were knocked off my face when I was wrestling with that fellow."

Elizabeth began picking up clothes and books, carefully searching through the confusion for his glasses as he explained what had taken place.

"I surprised them, coming in when they were going through our rooms. They took my passport and something from your room—I don't know what it was. My attempts to stop them only resulted in the girl knocking me out. Man, I don't know what she used, but she's wicked!"

"Didn't anyone in the hotel hear? Didn't someone come to help?"

"If they heard, they stayed away. It's an excellent case of *mai pen rai*—never mind. If it isn't your own troubles, never mind, just stay clear."

Elizabeth found his glasses under the desk, slightly bent but unbroken. She handed them to Martin and then sank down on the bed, unable to face the gravity of their situation.

"Did you by any chance learn their names?" Perhaps it was a foolish question in light of what happened, but it was the only one that came to her mind.

Martin adjusted his glasses and put them on, taking his time to respond. "Yes," he answered slowly, "his name is . . . Phil, and he called her Viv. Short for Vivian or Violet, I suppose."

"They'll try to get my passport, too, don't you think?" Her voice was calm, not expressing the dread she felt.

"It's likely," he replied.

"Then perhaps we should call the police."

"No, we can't. They've seen to that. The girl told me that the police were searching for them. And since we four bear some resemblance, they're going to use our passports to skip the country. They've already notified the police, anonymously of course, that we're in a hotel on this side of town. I don't think we would stand a chance if we called the authorities now."

"Why didn't they stay to get my passport, too?"

"Viv wanted to, but Phil got scared. He wouldn't stick around."

"What else did they say?" Perhaps he could remember something that would help them in their present situation, some clue as to where they could go for help, or at least, know who to avoid.

"They kept mentioning a Mr. Wong, and I think they were afraid of him."

"Wong?"

"Yes, I don't know who he is, but he's holding something over them, and they're trying to get out."

"Let's try to call Jonas at the airport." She looked at her watch, hoping he might still be there. "Wouldn't he enjoy knowing I want his help."

"He will be pleased, you know that. You'll have to try in the lobby; they cut our phone lines. But be careful."

Elizabeth took her purse, holding it close to her body to protect the passport inside—she would need it if the police came. Walking quietly down the long, narrow hallway, she jumped at every little sound; it was difficult to act normal when she was so frightened. She stopped just outside the lobby doorway to peer cautiously around, not wanting to walk straight into the arms of any military police who might have just arrived.

There were only two men in the waiting area; one at the

desk and one older Thai sleeping in a chair in the corner. Elizabeth walked hesitantly across the room to ask the manager for the airport telephone number. He helped her without question, then went back to reading the magazine that lay opened on the desk before him.

Wishing that he would be called out of the lobby so that he might not hear her conversation, she picked up the telephone at the far end of the long desk and dialed the number.

When the airport operator answered speaking in Thai, Elizabeth almost panicked, but with a silent prayer that the woman could understand English, she began a careful explanation. "I want to contact someone who is scheduled to fly out of Bangkok tonight."

The operator switched to English and Elizabeth explained that she would like to page a Mr. Jonas Adams. All the while she talked, she watched to see if the desk clerk was listening to her conversation. He seemed more interested in his magazine, but she still felt uneasy.

There was nothing she could do but elaborate on her request by saying that Mr. Adams' personal jet was to have left the airport a few minutes earlier, but she needed to contact him.

She went through the explanation three times before finding someone at the airport who could help. By this time, she was feeling desperate.

A man's clipped voice said politely, "I will check flight schedules. One moment, please." The line went silent, and for so long a time that Elizabeth was afraid she had been cut off. And Jonas' plane was getting further and further away from Bangkok.

Just as she was about to hang up, the man returned. "I am sorry," he said with a heavy accent, "but Mr. Adams' plane gone. No way to contact him now."

She could not ask that they try to get him by radio without fully explaining the circumstances, so she thanked the man for his trouble and slowly replaced the receiver. She glanced once more at the two men, but neither seemed the least bit interested in her. Frustrated and defeated, she turned and went back to Martin's room.

Her uneasiness was well-founded, however, for after she left the lobby, the manager made a telephone call to report what had just taken place.

"Well," she said, after reporting her failure to her brother, "what do we do now?"

"I've been thinking while you were gone. Perhaps we could get to Jonas' house tonight, and hide there while trying to get out of this mess. Tomorrow is Sunday, so we can't call Jonas' office—no one would be there. And I don't know where to contact Damrong; he thinks we'll be visiting the church where Dad was pastor. We could try to call the American embassy."

"But do you feel up to leaving?"

"We can't stay here waiting for the police to come and arrest us, can we?"

"No," she replied, finding the thought frightening. In just two days they had become fugitives, squeezed between the law and some sinister criminal element. She didn't dare let her mind wander to any fearful possibilities, knowing that the most important thing now was to get away from the hotel.

Martin stood up slowly, still feeling the pain of his recent encounter. "Well, let's use that shoulder bag of yours for what we absolutely need. Lock everything else in your suitcase. But do it as quickly as possible; I don't think we have much time."

Elizabeth tried to straighten her room as she hurriedly followed his instructions, but was so nervous she knocked over a perfume bottle and dropped her shoes twice. She took off the white orchid and her favorite blue dress and put on a pair of jeans and a knit shirt. Finally, she picked up her Bible and devotional sketch book from the floor, and put them, with a change of clothing, into the travel bag. Then she remembered the silver bracelet Jonas had bought for her just the night before. Strangely, she wanted it with her now.

Jerking open the desk drawer, Elizabeth reached down to retrieve the bracelet from its box. The drawer was empty.

"Martin," she said, perplexed and near tears, "they took the bracelet and spoon Jonas gave me. Why?"

"I don't know," he answered, his mind preoccupied as he moved quickly into her room. He was frowning and deadly serious as he shoved his things into the bag. Clearly he was upset, and this added to Elizabeth's apprehensions. She could not remember a time when he had not been calm, placid, and unruffled. Now he was worried!

When they were ready, Martin turned off the lights and they stood at the door, waiting for the right moment to leave. He looked cautiously down the hallway, but it was empty.

"Let's go," he whispered, pulling Elizabeth toward the back entrance of the hotel.

She glanced over her shoulder, half expecting to see someone in pursuit. "I hope it isn't locked," she said softly.

Martin reached out to try the door handle and Elizabeth held her breath. What would they do, if they couldn't escape unnoticed? "It's open," he said, motioning her on. "So far, so good."

Out on the veranda he reached for her hand and guided her down the steps and out toward the shrubbery. "We don't dare go around front."

And to confirm his reasoning, just as they melted into the darkness and cover of the trees at the edge of the hotel property, they heard a siren announcing the arrival of the police.

"Martin, won't they search the grounds, too?" Elizabeth's eyes were now adjusted to the darkness so that she could follow her brother without stumbling, but she stayed as close to him as possible.

"They might. So, we've got to find a gate in this fence!" His voice was low, but urgent. "Help me look, Liz. There ought to be one for garbage service, somewhere along here."

Wishing they could use a flashlight, Elizabeth felt her way along, trying not to fall over the debris stacked along the fence. Her foot hit a tin can, sending it rattling out of reach.

"Oh," she gasped. "I'm sorry, Martin."

"Never mind, I've found the gate."

It was locked, but it took him only a moment to pull the rotting wood apart so they might squeeze through.

Down the narrow alley, past crumbling service buildings and fences, they ran. Out on a side street they searched for an empty taxi or even a motorized *samlor,* but there weren't any. They would have to walk, trying to keep in the shadows of the shop awnings, dodging people and keeping an eye out for the police. Perhaps, Martin thought, it was best not to hire a cab, anyway; they didn't know who to trust.

After five blocks, Elizabeth stopped to put a steadying hand against a parked car. "Martin," she gasped, holding her side and trying to catch her breath. "I . . . I've got to rest!"

"OK, but over here instead," Martin said, and guided her into a darkened alley where they stood leaning against the building, both wondering if they would get to Jonas' house.

Just then Martin whispered, "Liz, there's a police car!"

The patrol passed slowly by, a light flashing along the shop front and down into the alley where Martin and

Elizabeth were hiding, crouched behind a wooden crate. It seemed like a lifetime—waiting for discovery—but the car moved on down the street and they both slumped back against the wall in relief.

"Now, if we can just be that fortunte the rest of the way," Martin mumbled. He picked up the travel bag and helped Elizabeth up from their hiding place and out to the sidewalk. The patrol car was no longer in sight.

After another ten minutes of alternately jogging and walking, Elizabeth was lost and disoriented. It seemed as though this section of town had more Chinese shops than she remembered.

"Are you sure we're going the right direction?"

"Yes," Martin replied, pulling her protectively to the left, away from a group of Chinese young men loitering in front of a restaurant.

Loud oriental music spilled out on the sidewalk, and the smell of peanut oil lay heavily on the night air. The traffic in the street sounded different from its American counterpart. Rain pummelled the scene with an intensity unknown outside a tropical country.

It was another world—sounds, smells, sights, all were foreign, and in the tension of their flight for safety, Elizabeth was thrown off balance. For the first time in her life, she felt alone, bewildered and out-of-place in Thailand. The rain streamed down her face, soaking her to the skin and pelting her almost to the ground. The Lord seemed far away; the world was dark and the forces of evil so close.

She was near panic and felt a scream forming in her throat. But, fearful of coming totally apart, she frantically pushed the terror down, forcing her emotions under a thin layer of control.

"M-Martin," she stammered, "where in the world are we?"

He glanced at her face, so strained and shadowed in the

slivers of street light coming through the unremitting rain. "Hang on, Liz. We're almost there."

The shops gave way suddenly to the quiet residential area where they hoped to find refuge. Elizabeth recognized several houses she had seen—surely not just that afternoon; there had been too many telescoped events, too many foreboding indications for this to have been just one day.

The quietness was not the comfortable silence of a neighborhood settling down for the night; to Elizabeth, it was the oppressive stillness of unseen eyes waiting, watching, stalking. Every tree and bush they passed were potential shelters for the enemy.

A car turned onto the road where they walked and Martin hastily pulled her behind a large, border hedge. They waited anxiously, wondering if it were the police or the unknown Mr. Wong. It moved slowly along, stopped before a house at the end of the block, and sat there for several minutes.

"They've stopped at Jonas' house," Martin whispered.

A man got out and walked onto the property, disappearing from sight as he approached the house. He was gone about five minutes, but it seemed like an hour to Elizabeth, who was beginning to get very worried.

"Do you think he's going to stay?"

"I hope not. I can't think of any other place to go at the moment," Martin replied wryly.

"Look, he's back at the car," she murmured, praying they would leave before she and Martin were discovered.

The sound of fierce barking nearby sent chills through Elizabeth, who was already shaking from the cold wetness of the rain and fear. If that dog was loose it would attack them in a minute.

What happened next seemed like an answer to her prayer. Lights went on across the street from Jonas' house, and voices could be heard as someone moved outside to investigate the noise.

Evidently, the men snooping around Jonas' house did not wish to be discovered; the car moved away, slowly and quietly, and turned onto the next road before flicking the headlights on again.

After a few minutes the porch light went off across the street and the night settled down into silence again.

"Now," Martin said, taking her by the arm, "let's get out of this rain."

"But will we have to break in?"

"No, Jonas gave me a key, just in case we wanted to move from the hotel."

They skirted the lawn, moving watchfully from tree to tree, dodging the open areas as much as possible. Then, Martin paused beside a low fan palm to take a look at the house. It seemed to be unattended, but he needed to confirm this if he could.

"Wait here, Liz. I want to do a little reconnoitering."

He disappeared, and the rain and the darkness pressed in on Elizabeth's dwindling confidence. If this weren't so serious, it would be the ultimate in the ridiculous—tiptoeing across the lawn and hiding like this. A small laugh escaped from her lips, and she realized she was near hysteria. Silently she prayed to the Lord and felt a calming spirit come into her mind.

And just about the time she was beginning to wonder if she ought to go look for Martin, he was back. "What do you think?" she whispered anxiously.

"I went all the way around the house. It seems quiet and empty."

"I hope so," she replied fervently.

They cautiously mounted the curving steps of the veranda, trying to be as noiseless as possible. Elizabeth held the travel bag while Martin carefully unlocked the door and slowly pulled it open.

Entering the darkened house was a partial relief; they were finally in Jonas' home, but they didn't yet know if someone was already there—waiting for them.

Martin took a small flashlight from his pocket and flashed it once, very quickly, around the room. There was no one, and they saw in that moment where they needed to walk.

He inched his way forward in the darkness with Elizabeth holding on to his hand and following as silently as possible. Then his leg hit the rattan couch he had been aiming for—the sound magnified in the empty house. He whispered in her ear, "Sit down, I'm going to check the rest of the house."

It was difficult for her to be there alone in the darkness, waiting for the possibility of someone attacking Martin, unable to hear his footsteps, seeing only a small flash of light as he entered the other rooms.

She jumped when he touched her arm. "Come on, I'll show you where the bathroom is. You can change your clothes and leave those wet things there." Holding his hand over the flashlight, he allowed only the slightest amount of light to escape—just enough for them to make their way down the hall. They did not dare turn any lights on, for fear of alerting others that the house was occupied.

The emotional reaction of their situation set off a fatigue she could not control and she continued to shake, even in dry clothes and wrapped in a blanket Martin had found. As she sat huddled on one of the twin beds in the guest room, drinking hot tea Martin had made, she said, "This is all my fault."

"Now, Liz, don't blame yourself just because you wanted to stay at the hotel."

"No, it is more than that," she said softly. They sat in the darkness, and she could see only a black figure sitting in the chair next to her bed. She wished she could see his face, could know his reaction to what she was about to say.

"What do you mean?"

"Well, when we went back to the hotel to rest yesterday—" she looked at the illuminated clock beside the bed. Yes, it was past midnight. "Yesterday afternoon, I found a note on my mirror. It said, 'We won't miss next time,' and . . ." She hesitated. "And, I also found one on the bench at the airport."

"Why didn't you tell me?" His voice was mild, unaccusing.

"Well, I was afraid you would tell Jonas, and I . . . I . . ."

"You're fighting him so hard, Liz. Why?"

She refused to answer, but went on as though she had not heard his question. "There is something else."

"What?"

"Well, it's not too important, but yesterday morning I wanted to sketch something in my book and the only clear thing that came to my mind was a picture of these two people we saw at the airport and that rod coming in through my window. It was almost like a warning."

"And you dismissed it from your mind."

"Yes," she confessed, "I just thought it was my imagination."

She was silent, allowing Martin to absorb what she had shared. Finally, she spoke once more, drawing her feet up under her as she turned toward him.

"I'm sorry, Martin. It's all my fault. If I weren't so pigheaded, we would not be in all this trouble."

He leaned over to touch her arm comfortingly. "Stop blaming yourself, Liz. I have a feeling this was going to happen, no matter where we were. There is something larger going on than two people chasing us. Let's just take one step at a time. Right now, we're here and safe. Now, let's get some sleep and then we'll try to get help in the morning."

It was difficult to settle down, but finally Elizabeth drifted into a fitful sleep of penetrating nightmares.

She was running down the dark streets of Bankok, trying to escape a group of Chinese men. They seemed to burst out of shop windows and leap from dark alleys—coming at her from every turn. Then she saw Jonas waiting at the next corner. He held out his arms and called, "Break down the wall, Liz. Come here, you'll be safe. Come!" She tried to get to him, desperately wanting the safety he offered, but just as she stepped off the curb, there was a terrifying sound . . .

So loud, she sat straight up in bed. "Jonas, no!"

Martin rolled off the other guest bed and came to her. "It's all right, Liz. It's just a dog barking."

"Wh-what time is it?" Her heart was jerking in reaction to her sudden wakefulness.

Martin reached over to pull the clock closer, squinting to see it without his glasses. "Almost four o'clock. It should be light soon. Go back to sleep."

She obediently laid back down, but could not stem the tumultuous thoughts that raced through her mind. What would they do if they could not make any contacts? Had they been followed? Was someone out there in the darkness waiting for an opportune moment to arrest or kidnap them? Why hadn't she listened to Jonas? And why did he have to be so dictatorial?

As she lay there trying to relax, she began to imagine scenes of arrest and incarceration in some filthy jail where they might be beaten or even shot to death. No one would come to their defense. Or perhaps, they would be kidnapped by some fearsome-looking Chinese who would slap her around and then sell her into white slavery, or deliberately force them into opium addiction and death.

In that moment, Elizabeth realized such thoughts did not help her to exercise faith. She absolutely could not succumb to the dubious luxury of trying to guess the future. She must believe what she had always been taught —nothing separates a Christian from God's loving care, not even the most trying circumstances. It was God's Word, and not to be questioned. It was the Psalmist who had written: "my heart shall know no fear . . ."

Then she slept.

She awakened two hours later to see the sun pouring through the lattice work that bordered the wall just below the ceiling. It scattered bright patterns over the shuttered room, and for a moment, threw her into confusion. Then she remembered where she was, and got up to look for Martin. Starting to call out, she remembered that any noise from this house could arouse the neighbor's curiosity or an enemy's interest. So she left her sandals by the bed and silently and cautiously padded out toward the kitchen.

"Good morning, Liz." Martin looked up from where he sat at the table in the center of the room. "How do you feel?" He kept his voice low, reminding her again of their precarious position.

" 'Morning. I don't feel too bad, considering our lack of sleep. How long have you been up?"

"About an hour. I wanted to check the house—as much as I could through the shutters. I don't think we've attracted any attention yet. Are you hungry?"

"Yes."

"There's fruit in the refrigerator and cold cereal and bread in the cupboard. I don't think we should use the stove—the aroma of food might make someone suspicious —but there is plenty of canned stuff in the pantry."

Elizabeth nodded in agreement and set about getting their breakfast. She marveled at such a modern kitchen in a traditional Thai house. But why should she expect to see a charcoal fire in Jonas Adams' kitchen? Concessions had been made to combat the ever-troublesome creatures found in the tropics—scorpions, house snakes, interesting ants and mice, to name a few—and the cupboards were well-insulated.

The back door of the kitchen led into an open area usually found in such homes, and she wondered if Jonas was native enough to put on a sarong and enjoy a cooling bath dipped from the large water pot in the corner. Here again Jonas had made changes by installing bars over the top of this open section, rather than leave it as an open invitation to thieves.

After they had eaten and prayed together, Elizabeth cleaned up the kitchen, working as quietly as possible, and then turned to look at Martin.

"Do you think Jonas would mind if I toured the house?"

"Of course not. He wanted us to stay here, remember?"

Just then the telephone rang somewhere in the house, and they both froze in their positions, looking at each other in frustration.

"We can't answer it, Liz. We don't dare give our position away."

"Where is it?" Elizabeth asked, wishing it would stop ringing.

"In Jonas' study—the first room behind the living room, across from where we slept."

They seemed locked into the sound, unable to move until it finally stopped. It was unbearable knowing it could have meant help for them. Perhaps Damrong had discovered they were missing, or the secretary was trying to find them with a message from Jonas.

Elizabeth sank down at the table, her troubled eyes asking more of Martin than he was able to give.

"Liz, I don't have the answers you want. I don't know what will happen." He brushed a few crumbs from the table and looked for a place to put the papaya peelings. "We know that this Phil and Viv have my passport and need yours, and they're tangled up with a Mr. Wong. And, the sure proof of our identification is in Chiangmai with our parents, or India with Jonas." He looked away, sorry that he could not be more encouraging.

"Apparently," Elizabeth said soberly, "the strength of my faith is about to be tested. Scripture says that nothing happens in our lives without God's permission."

"Not even a broken engagement?" he asked kindly.

Elizabeth looked up with a start. She hadn't thought of Peter since . . . since last night's conversation with Jonas, which seemed light years away. Actually, it had been more of a lecture than discussion.

"I don't know that I can say that yet," she sighed. "I should have followed the signs, but I chose to ignore them."

"What signs?" Martin asked. This was the first time she had shared much about her broken engagement; perhaps getting it out in the open would be therapeutic for her.

"Well," she replied, "he was never truly interested in anything about missions. If there were seminars or representatives on campus, he had other plans. I think he went to about three meetings with me. It was a disappointment."

"Were his reasons legitimate?"

"Sometimes. He did have a full schedule, but so did everyone else on campus. You would think that anyone who had such a professed interest in going to work overseas would find time."

"You aren't measuring his worth by his performance to

your set of standards, are you, Liz?"

"No. At least not in that instance. I was just perplexed then," her voice grew bitter. "Now, I understand." She frowned. "I don't mean that he had a total lack of interest, but he wasn't as involved as I wanted to be."

"Did you talk about it?" Martin pulled his glasses off and rubbed his eyes.

"Yes, but we never seemed to get anywhere. He would get angry that I questioned him, and so, I just dropped it. He went to the music concerts and films at school; I attended the mission meetings."

"Was your relationship a good one? Were you happy together?"

"At first yes. But after awhile, I began noticing things." She propped an elbow on the table, rested her chin on her hand, and stared out through the open area to the sky—it was going to rain again.

"What things?" Martin prodded.

"Well, he began standing me up a lot, but wouldn't mention what happened unless I asked. He always had some valid reason, but his apologies got to be rather flippant." She drew circles on the table with her finger. "The last few months, all he could talk about was *his* music, *his* concerts, *his* goals, and how much money he could make. He didn't even attend my student art show."

"Did you challenge him about his priorities?"

"No, I thought I was just reading into his actions things that weren't there. I was afraid I wasn't being fair, that perhaps I was just too narrow-minded about missions."

"And now?"

"Now? I'd rather be here in Thailand, and single for the rest of my life, than be treated like that again!"

"How has Jonas treated you?"

She sniffed. "He's so bossy!"

"Is he?"

Her eyes narrowed as she studied Martin's face. He was not teasing her; he was serious, so she told him what she thought. "Peter is an egoist, Jonas is a dictator! You should have heard him last night!" She told Martin what Jonas had said to her at the hotel. "He didn't soften the blow, either."

"Was he correct?"

"Yes," she admitted regretfully. "I am bitter, but don't I have a reason to be?"

Martin didn't answer, and she sighed. "I know, we may have a reason, but never a right." She was quiet for a moment. "If I really believe that God has a plan for my life, I shouldn't hate Peter for his actions. Why do I give God honor for the good things that happen, and then blame Him for the tough experiences?"

"We're all guilty of that, at one time or other." He could see her resentment was still strong, but knew that her guilt weighed heavily on her as well, so he said, "Liz, are you angry with God for our present situation?"

"No. I have a feeling things are going to get very bad for us, Martin; but I'm not angry."

"Are you afraid?"

"Yes," she admitted. "Are you?"

"Not yet," he grinned. He was not as prone to fantasize dark futures as Elizabeth, and she returned his smile, grateful for his calm spirit.

"What would I do without you, Martin? You know something? I'll miss you when you're flying for Jonas." *If we ever get out of the mess we're in now,* she thought.

He acknowledged her statement and said, "Jonas cares a great deal about you, Liz."

She shook her head. "He has known me all of two weeks. How could he have any strong feelings for me?"

"You know he does. Otherwise, I don't think you would fight him so. I've seen him look at you, and it's more than just a friendly concern. You couldn't find anyone in the world better than Jonas Adams.''

"No! I won't be hurt again! Why should I trust any man?'' She clenched her teeth and drew a deep breath. "I resent Peter's treatment of me. Why should he have such a good position with that company when he's treated me so badly? He doesn't deserve it. And about Jonas, isn't there a saying, 'Once burned, twice shy'? I guess that's the way I feel.'' She stood up—angry, but not sure where to direct the emotion and more than fearful at getting involved with someone else. She was simply afraid to trust Jonas Adams. "I'm going to look around.''

There were two rooms on each side of the hall that led from the kitchen to the living room—on one side, two guest rooms; on the other, Jonas' bedroom and study. Each had natural rattan furniture and its own color emphasis. The bedspreads and accessories where they had slept were made from beautiful blue Thai silks. Patterned batik material decorated Jonas' bedroom in subdued colors.

She walked leisurely and silently from room to room, recognizing the oriental beauty and the artistic appreciation of the owner of the house. There was a display of six delicate Chinese vases in a glass cupboard just inside his bedroom that took her breath away. Two vases on each shelf guarded gorgeously decorated silk fans.

She turned from the room, a little curious and certainly overwhelmed, to see this fragile display in the home of someone so obviously masculine as Jonas Adams.

Standing in the doorway of his study, she felt his presence even stronger, and it was threatening. Here she was struggling to keep him out of her life; and yet, his personality so stamped the colors and artwork, the books, the decorations, that her artist's heart was reluctantly opened toward him. She understood now why he wanted her to visit his home; he knew it would erase some animosity she felt toward him.

She moved to the glass case to read the titles of his books, noting the small lights inside which were used to keep books safe from mildew during the rainy season. There were histories of Thailand, well-known theological studies, biographies, business and economics, and at least a dozen books on art. She opened the door and took out an illustrated study of animals in Thailand and one of Thai arts and crafts.

Martin came to the door and glanced in. "Going to read?"

"Going to try. It will be unbearably hot in this house today, with the shutters closed." Holding up the books, she smiled slightly. "These might keep my mind off our situation." She stood beside him in the hallway, flipping through the pages of animal illustrations.

Martin put a warning hand on her arm and nodded toward the front door. She glanced in that direction and was alarmed to see the door knob turning. Neither of them moved while they watched the brass knob rotate back and forth. Then they whirled in the opposite direction—noises were suddenly coming from the back of the house.

"They're trying to climb in," Martin said close to her ear. He moved a few steps toward the kitchen and leaned over to look through the back door. Elizabeth was right behind him and saw a hand come over the top of the wall. Someone was actually attempting to break in, in broad daylight!

"Get in here," Martin whispered, pushing her into Jonas' bedroom and ducking in behind her.

"Did we leave anything on the table?" she asked in a low voice. "It would be a sure sign someone was in the house."

Martin shook his head. He had already anticipated trespassers looking for them and had put his coffee cup away before leaving the room.

The next events seemed to happen all at once, but it was probably her alarm that made it seem so.

They heard that same dog barking ferociously in the back yard and presenting a new and unwanted challenge to the wall climber, who tried to calm the animal, but only increased its protest.

A neighbor began shouting in Thai at the same time, warning the man to leave or the police would be called. The barking faded in the distance as he shouted—the dog must have the intruder on the run.

Hope began to rise in Elizabeth's heart that this situation was under control, until . . .

Until they heard someone open the front door of the house and walk into the living room!

"Jonas?" Elizabeth whispered hopefully.

But Martin shook his head and motioned for her to move behind the door. He picked up a heavy bookend as he followed.

Footsteps came quietly down the hallway and stopped. Two doors opened, for whoever was there was checking the study and a guest room. A soft tread on the floor came nearer, moving forward to Jonas' bedroom where they stood with eyes riveted to the door and hearts pounding. There was no place to hide, so they waited, helpless against immediate discovery.

Martin lifted the bookend as the door opened, slowly moving inward, inch by inch. A hand appeared. Just as Martin started to swing the bookend downward, a man stepped carefully into full view.

"Damrong!" Elizabeth cried softly in surprise. A flood of relief rushed through her and she moved to sink down on the edge of the bed. "Thank you, Lord," she whispered.

Damrong frowned and shook his head, a warning hand stopped her flow of words. Jerking his chin toward the front of the house, he signaled he was not alone. Someone waited outside.

"Sorry," Martin whispered, indicating the weapon still in his hand. "We're glad to see you!"

"I checked your hotel," Damrong replied softly. "Learned you are wanted by the police." He threw Elizabeth an apologetic look. "What happened?"

"That couple Elizabeth saw at the airport and sketched broke into our rooms, stole my passport and are after hers, too."

Damrong nodded grimly. "And they told the police that they were at your hotel," he guessed. With his current connections in Bangkok, he understood more than Martin could imagine and knew they were in deeper trouble than either of them could believe.

"How did you know?" Elizabeth asked.

Damrong shrugged his shoulders. "Typical," he said tersely.

"They spoke of a Mr. Wong," Elizabeth interjected.

Damrong's head jerked toward her, and she thought for a moment there was a flicker of surprise in his eyes, but it was difficult to tell. "Can't you help us?" she asked.

"I will come back tonight, as soon as it is dark, and get you to a safer place."

"But . . . but, can't you take us now?" Elizabeth knew that tonight would be too late; something was going to happen before then, she was sure. "Someone has already been checking the house."

He nodded. "I understand, but I'm sorry. The man who waits for me outside . . . he must not know you are here." He put out a hand pleading for their understanding. "I can't stay any longer; he will become suspicious. I am only supposed to be checking the house."

Elizabeth sat watching him with a feeling of uneasiness stirring within. He seemed more nervous after finding them than when he first opened the bedroom door. Somehow that seemed inappropriate, and she wondered if he felt they were a liability.

He backed out of the room. "Tonight," he whispered, and was gone.

They listened as he walked to the front door, heard it open and close and the lock snap into place. Then all was silent.

Elizabeth hugged the books she held and felt the perspiration gathering on her face and rolling down her arms. The tropical sun would bake them, unless it rained—but it was her nervous, uneasy feelings that affected her the most. "Why was he so nervous?"

"I don't know," Martin replied, replacing the bookend on the desk. "He certainly didn't want our presence known. I wonder who was with him."

"Martin, we should have asked him to contact the embassy or . . . or Jonas." A look of chagrin flashed over her face; knowing that Martin would feel she was becoming dependent on Jonas, and thus emotionally involved. "At least, he could give the authorities our proper identification," she said, then added hastily, "did you try to call the embassy?"

"No. I was coming to do that when the commotion started."

Elizabeth followed him into the study and waited while he found the telephone number and lifted the receiver to dial. "What's wrong?" she asked.

"Not a sound," he said, "nothing." Slowly he put the receiver back, staring at it thoughtfully. "Now all we can do is wait for Damrong."

Or an intruder, Elizabeth thought. "Perhaps it isn't dead, Martin. Try again."

He did as she asked, but there was no response. "I think the lines have been cut," he growled in disgust. "This is becoming a habit with us."

"Martin, do you think someone might still be here?" Elizabeth was worried and trembling as her imagination flicked through several fearful scenes that were possible.

"I'll check it out as best I can. We'd better be as quiet as possible, just in case. Try not to worry, Liz."

She nodded and sat trying to calm her imaginative mind as he left her alone. She was reluctant to leave the safety of the room, but finally stood and moved slowly toward the door. Glancing around the room she noticed a framed picture on a stand in one corner that appeared to be a wedding photo. Moving closer, she realized it was Jonas with a bride!

Stunned, she picked it up and studied the young woman —small and dark-haired, extremely pretty and radiantly happy. And the tender, loving look Jonas had for his bride made Elizabeth's heart skip a beat. He looked much younger, she thought, and wondered when the picture had been taken.

Now why hadn't he mentioned that he was married, or had been? And where was the young woman? She had not seen a wedding band on his finger. It was strange that he had not mentioned this in their long conversation about bitterness and tragedies.

Oddly, the emotion she was experiencing at that moment was not bitterness at all. She was jealous!

"No," she whispered in self-rebuke, and put the photo back in its place. Turning quickly, she looked toward the door, embarrassed to have Martin notice her reactions; but he was still checking on their safety.

They spent the rest of the day in quiet pursuits: sometimes reading, sometimes pacing, but always alert to any unaccountable sounds. They discussed trying to get to the embassy during the day, but Martin felt they should wait for Damrong. Elizabeth sat at the kitchen table for a while, trying to stay calm by drawing people who came to her mind.

First a small portrait of Jonas in one corner of the page, then one of Martin. In the third corner, Phil and Viv; and in the last corner, Damrong talking to the boatman who had interested her so. In the middle of the page she sketched in the floating market.

A lingering curiosity about the Chinese boatman compelled her to draw a larger picture of his face, then one of him in western clothes, and one in a Mandarin costume. And just for fun, she put Joy, Jonas' secretary, in a white, flowing wedding dress.

When she grew tired of working, she left the table and took the sketches to Jonas' study, and not really knowing why she had the urge to leave them on his desk beside the telephone, did just that.

After the evening meal her tension grew perceptible while they watched the sky turn dark with an abruptness that was always startling to a westerner. Elizabeth knew they would soon face danger; she just could not shake off a feeling of dread.

"Well, what next?" she asked. "I suppose we should be ready to . . ."

Her words were cut off, drowned in a sudden torrent of rain on the roof, and she could not even see the servants' rooms across the open area.

"I don't know if that is helpful or not," Martin remarked, looking at the downpour. "Let's get ready and wait in the living room."

He slipped into his shoes and started toward the front of

the house. Glancing at his sister, he asked, "Did you bring a sweater? It will be cold in this rain."

"No, we left the hotel in such a hurry, I forgot."

"Never mind. I'll see what Jonas has. I'm sure he won't mind."

Soon he was in the living room where she sat, straight and tensed. He threw a dark-colored sweater over the travel bag by the door and then sat down on the arm of the sofa next to her. "You can roll up the sleeves a few times," he whispered encouragingly.

She nodded and tried to return his smile, her stomach knotting with apprehension. "I wish Damrong would come!"

"So do I, but we must be patient."

By this time it was so dark that she could not see Martin's face clearly and so she reached out to take his hand and draw closer to him, staring into the blackness of the front door and wishing that anything—just anything—would happen. The suspense was worse than she could have imagined.

"I'm not very calm and patient," she said. "I wish . . ."

"Sh." Martin laid a finger across her mouth, and whispered in her ear. "I thought I heard something."

For a long drawn-out moment, they strained to hear any sound above the thundering rain, and when it came, Elizabeth's heart jerked in fear.

Someone began pounding loudly on the door.

Martin pulled her hastily to her feet and sped down the hallway, holding her hand and feeling his way along the walls. When they got to the kitchen, he said, "That can't be Damrong; he has a key."

For a split second, Elizabeth stood silently assessing their situation. If it was not Damrong, then it could only be Phil and Viv or else—Mr. Wong? She heard Martin moving about in the corner.

"Here," he said, taking her hand, "we'll use this umbrella and get back into the servants' rooms. If someone does break in, they may not look there. Or, if worse comes to worse, we could escape out the back."

He opened the umbrella and they dashed through the rain, pushed open a shuttered door and ducked into a darkened room. Elizabeth could not see a thing, and so she waited for Martin to close the umbrella and move forward.

"Liz," he whispered, "let's look for the back door."

"That not necessary," an accented voice said in the darkness.

Elizabeth gasped and then flinched as a strong flashlight flicked on, blinding them both so that they could not see who spoke.

A man moved into the light toward them, carrying rope in his hands, which he started to use on Elizabeth until Martin protested by taking a swing at him. A sharp command was given in Chinese and they turned to see a gun pointed to Elizabeth's head. "Stop, or I shoot," the voice ordered.

Her hands were tied behind her back and a handkerchief fastened roughly over her mouth. Martin received the same treatment, and his questions of why and who were not answered. The surprised encounter, the blinding light, the inability to see how many were there—everything was staged to subdue them quickly.

Someone took hold of her arm, yanked her out the door and down the steps to a waiting car that was pulled up close to the building. She was pushed carelessly into the back seat and Martin followed, landing in an angry heap beside her.

Her hands tied behind her back interfered with her balance and Elizabeth tried to find a comfortable position, but a third Chinese joined the group in the car, thrusting Martin over against Elizabeth as he crawled into the back seat, chuckling and speaking to his companions.

Martin and Elizabeth exchanged glances and she thought, with sudden clarity, this was the person who had pounded on the front door and sent them scurrying into the hands of his associates. And he was greatly amused at his success.

The car moved rapidly through Bangkok, avoiding the busier, heavily-traveled streets. Elizabeth saw neon lights flashing on store fronts and billboards that advertised movie stars and soft drinks in Thai and Chinese. She could hear radios blaring oriental and western music. She saw old Chinese men moving slowly along the sidewalk, and several young Thai men riding bicycles, umbrellas held over their heads. She felt dizzy as they moved from glaring street lights into darkened alleys and back again. The excessive number of turns meant that the driver was doubling back in order to confuse them and evade anyone who might attempt to follow.

She saw a street sign that read *Charat Road;* that was a district of Bangkok that was predominantly Chinese. She could tell by a pungent odor that they had just passed several open-air restaurants. The driver whipped the car into an alley, moved slowly down the narrow path, made a right and then two left turns, and then stopped before a large, darkened warehouse.

"Get out," the man beside Martin ordered.

They were pulled unceremoniously out of the car and propelled toward a small door which opened into a dimly-lit stairway.

In a few moments they were shoved abruptly into a surprisingly luxurious, second-floor office to stand before a man who was partially hidden from the small circle of light cast by a desk lamp.

Elizabeth could see a well-tailored business suit and darker, oriental hands. She moved nearer to Martin for comfort, and one of her captors growled and pushed her away.

"Do not treat her so harshly," the man at the desk said with humor and in perfect English, as he stood up and moved unhurriedly into the light. "I am sure our visitors will not give us any trouble."

Elizabeth's eyes widened in surprise and she glanced at Martin for his reaction.

She recognized the man standing before them! What had they gotten into now?

Five

Early Monday morning, Damrong sat in his office at *Adams Export, Ltd.,* impatiently watching the clock and chewing on his thumb. Jonas made a point of keeping in contact every morning he was away, but today his call was half an hour late. For the tenth time, Damrong looked at the telephone, willing it to respond to his urgency.

Frustratedly, he reviewed the previous day's activities, repeating each scene in an effort to discover what he could have done to prevent the consequences. He shook his head. He was in over his head, as the Americans say, and could only have done exactly as he had been ordered.

But that would not soften the news he waited to give to his employer, and Damrong felt he could guess what the reaction would be.

Jonas' two young American friends had come to Bangkok at the worst possible time; they were now going to be a definite handicap. The double existence in which he was now involved, and the ultimate outcome, could be in jeopardy because of them. He was in a difficult position as it was, since he thought highly of his employer, but still had to obey orders from others.

The telephone's shrill clamor in the silent building startled Damrong and he jerked up the receiver before it finished its first ring.

"Adams Exports," he said swiftly.

"Damrong," Jonas said cheerfully, "how are things at the office?"

"We are having some . . . account problems, Jonas," he answered carefully. They both understood the possibility of electronic surveillance, and had worked out a few simple signals. He had used one just now.

"Oh?" Jonas responded mildly. "What's wrong?"

Damrong drummed his fingers on the desk nervously. "One of your largest accounts was . . . fouled up over the week-end."

There was some static over the line but Damrong heard Jonas repeat his words. "Did you say 'largest accounts'?"

"Yes, that's correct. The one I have been working on for some time now," Damrong informed him.

"I see."

"However," Damrong continued, "I believe we'll have the solution any day now."

"Right," Jonas acknowledged. "I'll be back as soon as possible. Are you all right, Damrong? You sound pre-occupied."

"I'm fine, Jonas, fine." A false note of cheerfulness filled Damrong's voice.

"What about Martin and Elizabeth?" Jonas persisted. "How are they?"

"Well . . ." Damrong hesitated. He had his orders—get Jonas Adams back to Bangkok—and the news of the kidnapping would do it. But he was reluctant to share the information, things would go much smoother if he stayed in India.

Jonas was sharp and picked up his mood immediately. "What's happened?"

"They've . . . they've been . . . kidnapped."

"Kidnapped! How in the world . . . ? When did it happen?"

"Last night. I'm sorry."

For the first time in their association, Damrong heard anger in Jonas' voice, and he knew what his employer wanted to ask, but didn't dare. That would come later, when they could talk privately. "I think," he said, "that you had better come home."

"Right," Jonas agreed in a clipped voice. "I'll be there before the day's over. I can conclude my business here within an hour, if necessary."

"Good. Shall I meet you at the airport?"

"No. I'll contact you as soon as we arrive. And, Damrong . . ." Jonas hesitated.

"Yes?"

"I understand the importance of what is taking place, but, Damrong, she had better not get hurt," he ordered, his voice rough and threatening. "Do you read me?"

"I know, Jonas, I hear you." And he did, but he also knew someone who would not give her life a second thought if she interrupted his well-laid plans. He remembered seeing the body of his best friend lying at the edge of a rice paddy, with the sign of a red tiger on a scrap of paper clutched in his hand. No, there was a man in the city who would kill Elizabeth Thurston if she even looked at him wrong.

"I'll see you later today," Jonas said, concluding their conversation.

As Damrong stared thoughtfully at the receiver still in his hand, Joy came hurrying through the front door of the building, and seeing him there, called out, "Is that Jonas? Don't let him hang up. I've got something important to ask him.''

Damrong replaced the receiver. "Sorry, Joy, he was off the line before you came in. But, he'll be back sometime today. Can it wait?"

She stopped and turned to look at him questioningly. "So soon? I thought he would be gone most of the week. Is there anything wrong?"

"No, of course not," he responded a little louder than necessary. "He has done all he can in Bombay. You know the boss, once one job is taken care of, he is off on a dozen others. He's fine," he added, seeing her concerned expression. "Honest."

The thoughtful look she gave Damrong as she moved to her desk, reminded him again of how perceptive she was; she had sensed that something had indeed gone wrong. He would leave it to Jonas to tell her. "I've got rounds to make this morning to pick up some merchandise. I'll check in with you when I can."

"Fine. What time can we expect Jonas?"

He was nearly out the door before turning to answer her question. "I don't know; as soon as he can get flight clearance, he'll be on his way. See you later."

He heard her ask about Elizabeth and Martin, but ignored it, pretending he had not heard as he moved quickly to the van parked in front of the building.

Martin and Elizabeth had spent a restless night, locked in an airless, second-story room somewhere in the warehouse. There were two narrow, wooden beds in one corner, with the usual mosquito netting, a table, and five chairs. There was a Chinese calendar on the wall from which a dragon stared fiercely at the world. Two windows, shuttered against the night, provided the only access to fresh air. The ropes and gags had been dispensed with, but the guard would not allow them to talk much, so they were not able to encourage one another with more than a few whispered words.

It was a miserable night.

Breakfast had consisted of fresh fruit—some papaya and bananas—and hot tea. It was difficult to eat; knowing they were prisoners did not do much for the appetite.

Now the door opened and the guard motioned with his gun that they should follow him. "Come, boss want you."

He kept his gun trained on them as they walked down one hall and turned into another one in order to enter the richly-appointed office they had been in the night before.

And he was there again, sitting behind the desk, just completing a telephone call when they entered.

"Sit down," he said, motioning toward two chairs in front of his desk.

Martin and Elizabeth exchanged glances, and did as they were told. The two guards moved back to the door, where they waited patiently for their next orders.

"Miss Thurston," the Chinese said slyly, "It appears that you have recognized me. I salute your perceptiveness. Not many people notice me when I am . . . out of character."

Elizabeth merely looked at him, not caring whether or not he understood that it had only been her artist's awareness that had caused her to see through his disguise.

"Your sister knows," he said to Martin, "that I was the boatman who gave you a tour of the floating markets, and I expect she also has guessed at my true identity. I am Mr. Wong," he bowed mockingly before them. "I am the man interested in your passports." He motioned toward his desk and smiled sardonically. "In case you are wondering, I have them here."

"Then what do you want with us?" Martin asked quietly.

Elizabeth shook her head slightly and wondered how Martin could remain so calm and detached. She was bone-tired, in desperate need of a bath and fresh clothes, and increasingly aware of the sword dangling over their heads.

"Please," Mr. Wong smiled sarcastically, "all in good time. I do have plans for you, but first I shall answer your sister's unspoken question about my background." He seemed delighted that Elizabeth had such a sharp, inquisitive mind and turned to her—his dark, cold eyes making her shudder. He picked up a wicked-looking knife from the desk and ran his finger over the blade.

"I was born and educated in America, and after struggling through college as a hated foreigner, returned to Bangkok to run the import business I inherited from my grandfather. I have always been a true Chinese, loyal and enterprising on behalf of my people. I do not care for foreign influences in our beautiful city, and it is my goal to get rid of all of them." He paused, rising from his chair and walking silently around to stand near Martin.

"But," Elizabeth protested, "many Thai people consider the Chinese to be foreigners. There has always been trouble from strong ethnic feelings. Why do you speak of others as foreigners?"

"Listen to me," he said distinctly, overriding her words with his threats, and frowning at her insight. "By the end of this week, the *Adams Export* business will be eliminated, as well as . . ." he paused and smiled again, seeing her stiffen at his words, "as well as Jonas Adams, the owner."

"You are responsible for the threatening notes," Martin interjected thoughtfully.

"Yes."

"And the near accident with the boats?" Elizabeth added.

"Yes," Mr. Wong replied, pleased with their questions.

"Don't you think others know of your plans? I'm sure the police are aware of what you are doing." Martin challenged the man calmly, his hands lying quietly on his knees.

The Chinese grunted. "The police are most inept, Mr. Thurston. I know every move they make, and have allowed them enough information to keep them thoroughly confused."

"But Jonas is in India," Elizabeth blurted out, her mind still focusing on Wong's threat to kill him.

"It seems that he has discovered that you have been kidnapped, and is flying back to rescue you, my dear Miss Thurston. You have made quite an impression on him, haven't you?"

"And you're going to use us to hurt him," Martin said, suddenly realizing why they had not yet been disposed of. They were to be used as bait to snare Jonas, who somehow must be warned.

The man walked slowly over to Elizabeth and reached out to tip her face upward. "You are beautiful, for an American; I can understand why he is interested in you."

"Take your hands off me!" she said in a low voice, her eyes spitting fire.

But his hand only tightened, and she saw anger flickering in his eyes.

"Do you not care to have an oriental touch you?"

"It's not your nationality I dislike, it's your depraved mind!"

He released her chin, but his other hand moved up toward her face, until the gleaming knife rested gently on her cheek, and he murmured, "I wonder if he would still want you with a long scar on your face." And he drew the knife slowly across her skin, with just enough pressure to leave a red line.

She stared at him, refusing to allow her fear to show, holding his look until finally he grunted an acknowledgment of her strength and turned back to his desk.

She took a look at the knife in his hand then, shuddering at its sharpness, and saw that the handle was richly decorated with some sort of precious stones and a small red tiger. She glanced at Martin, whose face was white with anger and concern, and tried to smile reassuringly at him; it was a wobbly smile.

Then stubbornly she turned toward Mr. Wong; as long as she watched him, she could remain angry—angry enough to keep her mind sharp and unclouded.

A trickle of perspiration rolled slowly down her back despite the air-conditioned room, and she sat back, forcing her body to relax, thinking that perhaps Jonas' life depended on their actions now.

"How can you ruin his business?" she asked in disbelief, hoping to get him to talk. Somehow, they might be able to help Jonas, if only they knew Wong's plans. "There are too many people who have benefited from his help; they won't believe your slander." She felt Martin glance at her in surprise; here she was, repeating the very things he had been saying.

"They will believe the evidence," the Chinese said with a slight irritation in his voice. He was growing tired of their presence and questions.

"What evidence?" Martin asked.

Wong shifted his position and shrugged his immaculately clad shoulders.

"You don't want details, Mr. Thurston! I could never let you go free, with so much valuable information—could I?"

He turned suddenly and with one flick of his hand, sent that fearsome-looking dagger at one of his guards. Elizabeth gasped and Martin groaned in protest, each of them swinging about to view the results.

The guard was pinned to the wall, his face blanched white—the knife sliced right through his shirt sleeve, but he stood silently waiting for orders, his eyes never leaving his superior's face. Wong was teaching them a lesson and Elizabeth knew it.

"You have no intention of freeing us," she said.

Just then there was a knock on the door and at Wong's command, it opened and an old, raggedly-clad Chinese man stepped inside. Nervously wringing his hands, he spoke hesitantly to Wong, and while Elizabeth and Martin could not understand his words, the meaning was very clear. He was reporting some failure to Wong whose face grew thunderous as he sat with folded arms, staring at the old man, not saying a word when the stuttering speech finally trailed away. Suddenly, the old man dropped to his knees, his hands clasped together, begging for mercy. Slowly Wong pushed his chair back and reached into a desk drawer.

Elizabeth knew what he was going to do and her mind screamed rejection. "No, please don't!" she whispered, all the time knowing they were to have another lesson in the brutality of the man who held them prisoner.

He raised the gun and spoke a soft command, but the old man continued to moan as he crouched to the floor, until the guards forcefully pulled him up by the arms, making him stand to face Wong.

Elizabeth threw herself into Martin's arms just as the gun went off, catching a glimpse of the old man falling once more to the floor—but this time, he was dead. She heard Wong give another order, knew the door opened and closed, and still shaking uncontrollably, turned to see that they had removed the body.

A buzzer sounded on the desk and Mr. Wong calmly picked up the telephone, listened for a moment, gave an order and then hung up.

"I have an important meeting, so you must excuse me for interrupting our interesting conversation." He spoke without a hint of emotion in his voice, and Elizabeth turned to look at him.

"You're a monster!" she said tearfully.

He shrugged his shoulders and motioned for the guards, who had just returned to the room, to take them away.

They were watching the guard fumble with the door lock when they heard someone enter from the opposite end of the hallway, high heels clipping smartly on the wooden floor, and they looked up to see a young woman stop at the office of their captor.

Standing there, greeting Mr. Wong, she looked like a tiny Chinese doll, right from the top of her black hair piled high on her head, down to her tiny feet. She was dressed in a bright red, high-necked, traditional Chinese *cheongsam.* As Elizabeth's eyes took in the profusion of color, and she wished she could sketch her, she was startled and repulsed to see Mr. Wong lean over to give the girl a lingering kiss; it was definitely a very western greeting. Elizabeth shivered; one moment he was killing someone in cold blood; the next, kissing someone tenderly. He was a powerful man, one to be feared.

"Come," said the guard, jerking Elizabeth out of her musings to push her roughly through the door, threatening her softly until they were back in the room where they had spent the night.

She sank down at the table, her legs shaking with reaction to their confrontation with Wong, her head spinning and aching, and in a moment, her shirt was soaked with perspiration. "I hope it rains," she said in a shaking voice to Martin. "It might cool the air a little."

One of the guards opened the shutters, but warned them to stay away from the windows; then he moved slowly across the room and sat down near the door to talk with his companion.

Martin joined her at the table, pulled a small Bible from

his shirt pocket and began to read aloud.

"Where can I go from your Spirit?
Where can I flee from your presence?
If I go up to the heavens, you are there;
If I make my bed in the depths, you are there . . .
Your right hand will hold me fast. "

"What you do?" a guard demanded.

Martin turned and held out the Bible for their inspection. "I'm just reading."

The guards argued softly for a moment, until one shrugged his shoulders, and by his gestures seemed to minimize the activity, evidently telling his friend that it was harmless.

Martin continued to read from the Psalms, and then, in the same tone of voice and rhythm, and looking at the page before him, he said, "We'll escape when we can. Our friend must be warned."

Elizabeth's eyes slid over to the guards and back to Martin. They weren't listening, but she held her breath, hoping they would not notice.

Martin went on. "Don't give up looking for our chance. One friend is aware of our situation and must be trying to help, so we'll . . .

A sharp knock interrupted his words, and Elizabeth tensed, expecting to be taken back to face Wong again. They watched silently while a guard unlocked the door to welcome the very two people who seemed responsible for their predicament.

"The boss wants you two," Viv said to the guards, and pulling a gun from the jacket slung over her arm, she leaned against the wall and stared at the two prisoners.

"Well, Phil," she said after the guards had gone, "there's one for you," pointing the gun at Elizabeth, "and one for me," pointing it at Martin.

Phil sent Elizabeth a regretful look, his eyes asking for

indulgence of Viv's actions. He sat down, ignoring the comment and seemingly preparing himself to do only what he had been ordered—guard the door.

But Viv was ready for some amusement. She pushed her shoulders from the wall and sauntered over to the table, her movements as sensuous as possible, her expression expectant as she watched Martin.

"Reading the Bible!" she said, her surprise killing her provocative intentions for the moment. "You've got to be kidding!" She pulled the book from his hands and tossed it on the table, then turned to look at him closely.

But his blatant look of disinterest pricked at her pride with thorn-sharp accuracy, and her arm pulled up, pointing the gun into his face. She would show him who was in control.

Phil shot forward in his chair. "Viv," he warned quietly, "watch your temper. Wong could walk in here any minute."

"I don't care," she retorted, tossing her head.

"Well, I do. Come on, Viv," he pleaded softly, "stop it."

"Shut up!" she responded, turning from Martin to look at Elizabeth, her face full of scorn, her laugh cynical. "Well, well, little sister, fresh out of college and ready to take on the big, bad world. Did you come out here to save the orient? You should start with Wong—before he kills us all."

She pulled a chair around as she talked, pushing it against the wall with her thong-covered foot, and then sat down. Her faded blue jeans and sleeveless knit top looked as worn as the tired expression in her eyes.

"What do you think you can do, little Miss Innocence? Coming out to Thailand to flaunt your religious hypocrisy. Why? Why didn't you stay where you would be safe?" Viv twisted around in her chair in growing disgust. "What makes your religion any better than what these people have been practicing for hundreds of years?''

"We don't practice a religion," Elizabeth answered.

"No?" Viv pulled a leg up on her chair and propped the gun against her knee, keeping it trained on Martin.

"No," Martin said. "We have a relationship with Jesus Christ, who sacrificed His life and died so that every human being can have eternal life."

Elizabeth took a quick look at Phil; he seemed sincerely interested. However, it was but a momentary diversion for Viv who swore at them—gutter language spilling from her mouth like dirty water from a polluted river. "Religious nuts," she said dismissively.

"You don't seem to be doing too well on your own," Martin offered kindly. "Why not try Jesus Christ?"

"Sounds like a TV commercial for a better detergent," Viv smirked. "Besides, you two aren't exactly on vacation at the moment. If Jesus knows you personally, how come you're in so much trouble?"

"Being followers of Christ doesn't exempt us from trouble," Elizabeth replied.

"What does it do for you then?" Viv demanded.

Elizabeth thought for a moment. She needed the right words—simple and clear—for she was sure Viv would terminate this conversation momentarily. It wasn't something the girl really wanted to hear.

"Well, Christ promises to go through our problems with us. Sometimes, we are delivered; sometimes not. But always He gives strength and courage."

"Have you got a man?" Viv asked, suddenly changing the subject.

Elizabeth's face mirrored first surprise and then resentment, then became a mask of confusion.

"What's the matter—did he dump you?" Viv laughed, enjoying Elizabeth's spontaneous, silent acknowledgment and chagrin. "Can't your Jesus help you get a man?"

"Viv," Phil broke in, his voice mild, "that's enough. Leave her alone."

Elizabeth shot Martin a look of painful apology; she hadn't realized her emotions would surface so easily. But Jonas had been right; you can't nurse your resentments in hiding. They always spill out in unguarded moments. Here she was, so full of bitterness over the past that she was unable to share any kind of positive statement with this girl.

Viv slanted a mocking look at Phil. "Do you want to become her knight in shining armor? It's the kind of thing you're suited for." She spoke sarcastically. "You might make a good substitute—the answer to her maidenly prayers." She laughed, having succeeded in discomforting the two. Phil's face was red and he looked ready to strangle her; Elizabeth stared at the table in defeat. Viv glanced at Martin, expecting to see the same embarrassment, but his thoughtful stare pierced her thin armor of worldliness to touch her own anger and fear. Her superior mood vanished and she silently vowed reprisal against him for reaching the vulnerable spot she had always kept hidden.

"Well, superman," she said, lifting the gun to remind him of the power she had, "how about being my man? Maybe we could escape together."

"How do you plan to do that?" Martin asked, curious about what she had in mind.

"I know where Wong keeps your passports, and the first time he is away from that office, I'm going to steal them. I'd rather take you with me than Phil; he's a vacuous bore." She turned to see what affect her words were having on Phil and laughed at his discomfort. "He hates to hear me talk like this. Don't you, Phil dear? Well, superman, is it a deal?"

Martin shook his head. "No thanks. I'll stay with Liz. We either get out of this together, or not at all." He reached across the table to give his sister's hand a squeeze.

Viv saw the gesture and was suddenly envious of such devotion, in spite of having ridiculed and rejected any from Phil. She did not understand the force that drove her to reject love in order to flee to such peaks of hatred, but looking back over her life, she decided it had developed gradually—becoming a meaningless pawn in Wong's plans had been only the final straw. She did not think there was any room in her soul for love—of any kind—and that drove her relentlessly forward to mock any indication of affection, wherever she could. She had to strike out at others, had to destroy just as she was being destroyed. There was no peace nor satisfaction in anything less. The irony of it was, that even in destruction she felt an unfulfilled rage.

She raised the gun and pointed it at Martin, so possessed with the need to obliterate the peace and stability he exhibited that her hand shook.

The others in the room sat immobilized, fearing that any move would force her to pull the trigger.

"Oh, Lord," Elizabeth prayed silently, "stop her, please! Do something!"

Martin stared into Viv's eyes, silently demanding that she lower the gun.

His expression startled her, for she had expected—had wanted—him to display a gentle kindness that would give her cause to hurt him. But to see this steadfastness was unnerving and she faltered, finally letting her anger seep slowly out of her body.

Then she laughed—a hollow sound that bordered on hysteria. "Well, you passed the test, superman. You didn't flinch." She lowered the gun and asked Phil for a cigarette. "I wonder if you'll show that much courage when you face Wong's gun," she said to Martin.

"Will it come to that?" he asked, trying to get more

information from her.

Viv shrugged her shoulders and blew cigarette smoke straight toward him, her hand shaking slightly from the violent feelings she had just experienced. "It might. Some of Wong's opponents have ended up in the river; others just disappear."

"What does he want from us?" Elizabeth asked, fanning herself with a Chinese magazine from the table and feeling slightly dizzy.

Viv threw her a condescending look. "He's planning on ruining some foreigner's business, so he can become more powerful."

"How?" Martin shifted in his chair to a more comfortable position, ignoring Viv's warning reaction with the gun.

"I don't know. Maybe plant opium in his warehouse; maybe pin a murder on him. I don't know what he'll do, but you can be sure it will be a fool-proof plan."

Martin continued asking questions, hoping for information that would help them escape and thwart Wong's plans for Jonas. Dying at the hands of a gangster wasn't exactly what he wanted either, so they had to find some way out.

Viv didn't seem to know the timing of Wong's plans, but thought it would probably be within the next twenty-four hours. Keeping two Americans as prisoners for any indefinite time was not practical, especially, she said, since they were so diametrically opposed to becoming a part of Wong's efforts—even just to save their own skins.

"What else have you heard?" Martin asked again.

"I don't remember," Viv responded in irritation.

"I do." Phil spoke, ending over an hour of silent observation and the others jumped at his voice.

"What?" Elizabeth questioned eagerly.

"There is an employee at Adams Ltd., who is working for Wong. I'm sure he is prepared to plant opium somewhere."

"Just finding a drug in his warehouse would not prove anything," Martin said.

"It would if it was hidden in some of the merchandise," Phil responded.

"Yes," Martin agreed reluctantly. "And, if there was enough of it there, it would appear to be a drug operation."

A picture suddenly flashed into Elizabeth's mind and she frowned, thinking of Damrong's concern over the silver spoon Jonas had given her. Was he the traitor? No, it just couldn't be. Perhaps, it was the man Damrong had been arguing with the day she was in the stock room.

"What is it, Liz?" Martin asked.

"Nothing." She did not want to accuse anyone falsely, and wanted desperately to give Damrong the benefit of the doubt, for if he was really guilty, Jonas was in deep trouble.

Martin stood up and slowly paced the room, still ignoring the gun that Viv persistently waved in his direction.

"What's the matter, are you getting nervous—cracking a little?" she jeered.

"No, just stiff from all this inactivity."

The day went by slowly and miserably. Elizabeth's mind grew weary of Viv's vindictiveness and the constant threats on their lives; she felt dizzy with fatigue. Martin looked tired, but was still able to question Viv and even had a long conversation with Phil about the Lord.

Viv mocked everything he said and made herself so obnoxious that Elizabeth began to wish she might come to some harm. If only she would be quiet. Oh, how her head ached from the heat and tension; how she wished for a cool bath and a long, long sleep!

Finally, just as darkness came, one of the Chinese guards arrived and spoke hurriedly to Phil.

"Boss want you two," he said, motioning toward Viv. His hand was shaking slightly and he was extremely agitated. "Hurry!"

A moment later, Elizabeth and Martin were alone, and they sat savoring the silence and absence of constant threats and mocking words.

"Must be a snag in the works," Martin observed softly. "They forgot to leave a guard."

"Unless they are in the hallway."

"Perhaps, but I doubt it." He got up and went to the door. Turning the handle, he rattled it a little. "It's locked, and if there was a guard he would react to this protest." He pushed against the door, trying to find a weak spot, a way of escape.

Elizabeth stood up and moved to the barred windows, seeking any small breeze to cool her face. She felt unnaturally hot and extremely weak. Her legs buckled and she caught hold of the window sill. Turning, she started to say something to Martin, but the room tipped to one side and a loud buzzing sound went off in her head. She staggered to the table and fell into the chair.

"Martin, I don't feel well. Oh, my . . ." It felt so good to rest her heavy head on her arms folded on the table.

Martin felt her forehead. She was burning up and there was nothing he could do; they had no medicines. It was probably that bane of the tropics—dengue fever—and it would run its course. He prayed it would be a light case, for he didn't want her out of her head and unable to respond should they have opportunity to escape. He poured a glass of water from the pitcher left from their noon meal. "Here, try some water. Hang on, Liz, don't go under."

She smiled weakly. "I'll try not," she responded. "Oh, I ache all over! This would have to happen now. I'd better lie down, Martin.''

He helped her to the narrow cot in the corner and she sank down, grateful to be in a prone position, to slow down the merry-go-round in her head.

"If we just had some aspirin, Liz. That would at least relieve the aches a little.''

Hearing the sound of a key in the door pulled their nerves out as taut as a violin string. Both visibly relaxed as they watched an old Chinese grandma enter with their supper on a tray and the key to the door on a chain which she had twisted around her wrist.

She was tiny, with white hair pulled severely back in a bun, and dressed in a black cotton top and black, full skirt-like trousers. Her face was so full of wrinkles there wasn't room for another. She kept her eyes averted, not wanting to acknowledge their presence in the room.

Martin moved nearer as she put the tray on the table, and speaking in Thai, asked if she would help them escape. She did not respond, so he asked if she spoke Thai. The old woman shook her head and frowned.

Then he tried again, suggesting that she might help by leaving the door unlocked. Anything might help. They needed to get away, quickly, before the guards returned.

At each request, the old woman shook her head and grumbled at him, getting more agitated as he pressed her. Finally she picked up the tray from the noon meal, and started toward the door.

As Elizabeth tried to sit up to add her plea, the old woman glanced at her for the first time, and realizing she was ill, hobbled slowly across the room to feel Elizabeth's forehead, shaking her head and mumbling in Chinese— probably trying to give them some medical advice which they would be unable to follow.

Elizabeth caught hold of her hand and pleaded, "Help us. Help us, please!''

But the old woman jerked her hand away, and with fear in her eyes, muttered again in Chinese while waving toward the place where Wong's office would be. Significantly, she pulled her hand across her throat and grunted.

"Yes, yes," Martin agreed. He understood she would be taking a great risk, but what else could he do? Once more he requested her help, reaching out his hand for sympathy, but she jerked back and turned toward the door. Shuffling across the room, her back bent with the length of her years, she muttered to them in a steady, angry stream of Chinese. At the door, she turned and shook her head again.

The door slammed behind her small figure and they waited in silence to hear the key turn in the lock; but all they heard was the old woman's voice, now raised in strident tones, fussing angrily as she walked away.

"Martin, didn't she lock it?" Elizabeth struggled to stand up, her body drenched in perspiration.

He stepped to the door and cautiously tried the handle. It rotated easily in his hand, and he pulled it open, looking out into the hallway.

"Nobody is here, Liz. By accident or design, she did just as we asked! Let's go!"

They hurried silently down the hallway, looking for any means of escape from the building, expecting guards to be waiting at every turn. They tried every door, but each one only opened into another room and all the windows were barred. It looked as though the only way to escape was the stairway just outside Wong's office, and they were sure to be caught if they went that way. Finally, Martin opened one more door, and it was what they had been searching for; it opened onto a stairway, which led out a back entrance. At the bottom of the steps they found another obstacle—a locked door, and at the same time heard voices shouting from upstairs. The guards had discovered they were missing—they had only seconds to get out of the building before being caught.

Martin put a shoulder to the door frame and slammed hard, but it did not budge. He tried again, several times, before it finally split and gave way.

"They must not have expected any trouble; this door isn't very strong," he said as he pulled Elizabeth through and out into the darkness. "Come on, we're getting away from here!"

They hurried along the back wall of the warehouse, hugging it like a lifeline, watching for any guards that might be posted around the premises.

In the silence they could hear the river lapping against the wooden piers at the water's edge; but the shrubbery was so thick, there seemed no way through. At the back corner, they stopped while Martin took a cautious look around the side of the building. Then he ducked back. Two figures had broken away from the building front, talking excitedly and scurrying around, searching for them.

"We can't go that way," he said, trying to figure out how to get by the guards to the main street and hopefully, to freedom.

Elizabeth leaned against the building. She was too weak and her mind too foggy to walk much further or make any suggestions. They had a long way to go to safety, she thought, and it seemed like a momumental task.

"The river," Martin said suddenly, grabbing her hand and pulling her toward the water. "Maybe there is some kind of boat tied up nearby."

It was so dark that neither of them could see very well, and Martin ran straight into a line of bushes, grunting softly as the branches tore at his face. "Watch out, Liz!" he whispered, but it was too late. She had staggered straight into the limbs as he tried to catch her. "Here, let me help you." He put a supporting arm around her waist to give her strength.

They worked their way slowly through the bushes, Martin holding Elizabeth as they pushed and pulled, feeling the limbs pulling at their clothes and scratching their arms and faces. They worked frantically, knowing the guards would soon be at the back of the building; perhaps were even there already. Martin had to do most of the work; in the darkness Elizabeth was more disoriented than she wished to be. Finally, they stood at the river's edge and staring out in the darkness, saw the outline of a boat bobbing quietly in the water.

"I think we're going to make it, Liz! We can get away faster on the river than going by the streets."

They heard the guards rounding the back of the building, and saw flashlights slashing into the darkness to aid their search. Martin helped her up on the pier and they ran silently out to the boat.

It appeared to be safe. No one seemed to be around, and that was what they needed. There was a canvas covering over the back half which would hide them from observers on the shore once they got out into the river.

"Thank goodness," Elizabeth whispered and almost fell into the boat, her legs refusing to hold her up any longer. She sank down on a seat and waited for Martin to untie the rope and push them out into the current. They were so near to safety.

Suddenly a strong searchlight from shore flicked on and caught them both in its light, framing them in stark whiteness and futility. At the same time two men stepped out from under the canvas cover at the other end of the boat.

"Damrong!" Elizabeth cried out in relief, almost sobbing. "Help us quickly! Get the boat away before

Wong's men get here!''

But he just stood there, watching them with that inscrutable expression on his face and Elizabeth was appalled.

Martin swung around from untying the boat and looked at Damrong, then noticed that the man next to him held a gun, pointed in their direction.

"Damrong," Elizabeth cried, almost in tears, "Please!"

"He isn't going to help us, Liz," Martin said sadly. "I'm sorry, but it seems that Damrong isn't on our side."

"Why not? What do you mean?" Just then she, too, caught sight of Damrong's companion, her eyes moving down to the gun in his hands, and then she looked once more at Damrong. "No," she cried out, and in defeat, slumped over in a dead faint.

Six

It had taken Jonas longer to get out of Bombay than he had anticipated, and once his jet was in the air, he couldn't sit still. He was restless in his concern for Martin and Elizabeth, and made so many trips forward to check with his pilot—trying to put more speed into their flight—that the young man threatened to lock him in the bathroom, just to keep him off his back.

At seven o'clock that night, just as Martin and Elizabeth were making their escape attempt, the plane landed at the Bangkok airport, and Jonas made a determined dash for the first telephone he could find.

He dialed the office number; no one was there. Then he tried to reach Damrong's home.

"Answer the phone!" he muttered, as if his frustrated command would be obeyed. Finally, on the eighth ring, he hung up and stared at the telephone as though it had insulted him.

He called his home and got no response at all. What was wrong with his telephone line? He had had trouble before with poor service; was this the problem now, or . . .?

He called the hotel where the Thurstons had been and was informed that they were not in their rooms.

"How long have they been out?" he asked the desk clerk.

"I am sorry, Sir. I do not know."

"Did they leave any messages?"

"No, Sir."

"Did they leave word when they would return?"

"No, Sir."

Jonas curled his hand into a fist, wanting to put it through the wall. Instead, he thanked the clerk and hung up.

With growing frustration he tried Damrong's home number again, calling three times before finally giving up. Where was Damrong? What was he doing? He was always available when Jonas returned to Bangkok—either waiting at the airport or the office. Now Jonas was afraid that he was in trouble also.

He walked swiftly across the lobby, waited impatiently as a policeman checked his passport, and then got into the first taxi outside of the terminal and gave his office address.

"Put wings on this thing," he told the young Thai. "This is an emergency!"

It was a job the driver plunged into with tremendous zeal, just the thing he enjoyed—transporting an important customer, making a trail of smoke as he darted in and out of traffic, blowing the horn constantly, and missing other vehicles by a breath's length.

And for once in his life, Jonas was blasé about the dangerous drive he was taking; his mind was on the kidnapping. He didn't even respond when the driver took both hands from the wheel—still going full speed—and folded his hands in a sign of prayer when he passed a temple noted for protecting travelers.

When they finally pulled up in front of his office twenty minutes later, Jonas leaped out before the taxi had fully stopped. "Wait here," he said, flinging the order over his shoulder.

He unlocked the front door, flicked on the display room lights and began a quick search for his assistant, calling his name loudly, but receiving only silence for an answer. He opened the stock room door and stepped inside. It seemed quiet, but in the dim night light, Jonas called out hopefully, "Damrong, are you in here?"

"Where *is* that guy?" he muttered.

Frowning, he ran up the stairs to his own office, thinking there might be a message on his desk; but it was just as he had left it, except for a pile of correspondence Joy had left neatly stacked on one corner. He tossed his briefcase on the desk and stared at the floor, trying to think of what he should do. He was running into one wall after another, and he cried out to the Lord for guidance. He had thought so little about the threatening notes, feeling he could take care of himself. But to have his friends in danger was something else.

"Lord, show me what to do," he whispered. "I feel utterly helpless."

He retraced his steps out to the taxi and gave the driver his home address, hoping that when he arrived, Damrong would be there with news of the Thurstons. He had a strong feeling that his assistant would know where they were and how to help. It's funny, he thought, but for the first time in their relationship, he was leaning on his Thai friend—and at the moment, felt lost without his presence.

When they arrived at his home, he paid the taxi driver and took the veranda steps in three strides. Unlocking the front door, he stepped inside and, in the darkness, tripped over some object just in front of the door. Flipping on the light switch, he saw it was a large shoulder bag—Elizabeth's—with his own sweater thrown over the top. This tangible evidence of the Thurston's presence in his home slammed the reality of the kidnapping right into his face. He took a deep breath, trying to channel his emotions into positive steps that he could take. *Look through the house,* he thought; *maybe there is some clue of who took them, or where they are now.*

The covers were thrown back on one of the guest room beds, someone had used the stove and taken food from the refrigerator, and the wedding picture on his night stand had been moved. He even went through the two servant rooms at the back where he found a discarded umbrella, which he picked up and returned to its place in the kitchen. There didn't seem to be any signs of struggle anywhere, yet Jonas felt strongly that they had been abducted from his house.

When he entered his study to try to contact Damrong again, everything seemed in order and he sat down behind the desk and reached for the telephone.

"I might have known," he muttered when there was no dial tone, "the line has probably been cut."

He dropped the receiver back in its place in frustration, and started to leave the desk when he happened to glance down to see the drawings Elizabeth had left there. Sitting down slowly, he picked the papers up and turned them around; a compelling longing for her swept over him and he rebelled at the possibility of never seeing her again.

Then he smiled wryly—his picture didn't have heavy black lines slashed through it. That was progress. there were sketches of Martin and Joy, a small one of Elizabeth, and even the two young people from the airport, but he was puzzled by the Chinese boatman and the fact that Elizabeth had drawn him a number of times in different costumes and poses. She must have been fascinated with him for some reason.

There was a small nagging thought in the back of his mind as he sat staring at the work she had done. Had he seen this Chinese before? His face seemed familiar, and it was apparently important to identify him—particularly since he wanted any lead he could find. He searched his mind, rejecting the mental images of men at the Chinese club, at the bank and at church; none of these seemed to pinpoint the man. He just couldn't come up with an answer. Perhaps it was just a composite of people she had seen.

He glanced at his watch. It was late, past a respectable hour for troubling the chief of police, but that wasn't going to deter him. This was too urgent to wait until morning. Standing up, he slipped the pictures into a small briefcase, found his car keys, and left the house.

Traffic was still heavy—the streets full of vans, tour buses, and private cars, all carrying tourists and local people on a search for the exciting night life which Bangkok offered. He tried to be patient as he maneuvered his way downtown to police headquarters, but it wasn't easy.

"Come on, let's go!" he kept ordering the traffic, then braked quickly to avoid the car in front of him and shook his head. After living in Southeast Asia for five years, he thought he had adopted some oriental patience, but it had evaporated in his anxiety over the kidnapping.

The officer on duty at the front desk was polite but firm. The Chief, usually not in the station at such a late hour, happened to be in an important meeting and could not be disturbed, especially by a foreigner, his manner seemed to say. Foreigners were always in a hurry because they thought their business was so important.

Jonas talked persuasively, explaining that he had friends

in grave danger and he needed help, but it wasn't until he gave his name that the officer responded favorably.

"Oh, Mr. Adams," he said with a big smile, "you are famous in Bangkok. My mother was cured at your clinic. She had been going to doctors for years . . ."

"The Chief . . ." Jonas interjected hopefully, but he wasn't heard.

"Probably about ten years . . . no, it was more like eleven—with an undiagnosed problem. She even went to medicine men and the Buddhist monks, seeking relief."

"The Chief, I need to see him," Jonas repeated. At any other time, he would have enjoyed the talkative, likeable officer, but not tonight!

"I must say, you have some of the best doctors in the world at that clinic. I have given thanks to the Lord Buddah every day for her recovery. It was so terrible, she lost so much weight, and we just did not know what . . ."

Jonas waited impatiently for the officer to take a breath, to stop the words pouring out of his mouth in praise of the help his mother had received.

"Ah, young man . . ."

The officer continued. "I remember one night we had almost given her up for dead. She had not eaten for two weeks, and was hallucinating. That was when we decided that something had to be done . . ."

He paused for a breath and Jonas jumped in. "I'm grateful for your praise of the doctor's work, but I really must see the Chief now."

"Oh, yes, yes, of course," the officer said agreeably.

Finally, after forty-five minutes of pacing the floor and praying, Jonas was relieved to see another officer enter the room and beckon him to come. He was ushered into the office of Prince Chandruang, Chief of Police, and after the customary polite greetings and preliminary small talk, which could sometimes last nearly an hour, the Prince finally asked Jonas the reason for his visit.

"I'm sure," Jonas began, "that you're aware of the problem I'm having in my business."

"Yes, the Red Tiger has been sending threatening notes to you, has he not?" The Prince, a distant relative of the King, spoke in a slow, measured voice. He sat down behind an expansive, uncluttered desk, and after offering a cigarette to Jonas, which was refused, leisurely lit one for himself.

He was impeccably dressed, his elaborate uniform smooth and unwrinkled, and hiding a slightly rotund figure. Even his movements behind the desk were methodical and organized, not one ash fell from that cigarette to the floor. Jonas felt untidy and disarrayed, like a school boy caught playing in his best clothes, and he was disconcerted as he prepared to present his appeal.

"We have one of our best men on this case," the Prince said. "One of your close friends."

"Yes, I know, but I wonder if you realize that someone kidnapped an American employee of mine and his sister."

Not even a slight frown marred the Prince's well-set expression. "That is unfortuante, but I am at a loss to understand what one problem has to do with the other." He straightened a fountain pen and pad next to the telephone, waiting for Jonas to get to the point.

"I'm very anxious to find them before something tragic happens!" Jonas felt his voice rising in his desperation to get action. "They were kidnapped last evening, from my home."

"And you would like us to begin a search for them?"

"Yes, by all means!" Jonas exclaimed, then remembered that he was speaking to royalty—though far removed from the palace. "I would be most grateful for your help."

"Of course, my friend, we shall begin immediately," the Prince replied with typical unruffled calmness. Jonas clenched his jaws and wondered if he would ever become accustomed to the absolute control of emotions most Thais displayed.

"But, you must remember," the Prince warned, "there are many places in this city where two Americans could be held hostage."

Jonas nodded, thinking of the hundreds of buildings along the river and the Chinese boat houses, not to mention hundreds of little hovels he had never even seen.

"Can you give us a description of your friends?"

"Yes," Jonas answered as he drew the sketches from his briefcase. "Martin is about my height, slim, light brown hair, wears wire-rimmed glasses." He handed the pictures to the Prince and paused as the word beautiful came to his mind when he thought of Elizabeth, but that would hardly be helpful to the police.

"Martin's sister is about 5' 4", has short brown hair, and . . ." he smiled slightly, his eyes clouding over as he thought about her, ". . . and a model's figure."

The Prince nodded, one eyebrow raised at the description, his eyes studying Jonas' expression. Then he looked down at the sketch. "She is beautiful" he said, agreeing with Jonas' unspoken assessment.

"Were the Thurstons guests at your home while you were away?"

"They had been at the Hotel of the Beautiful Palms, registered there on Friday."

"Then, why were they kidnapped from your home?" Prince Chandruang picked up his pen and wrote a few notes on the pad in front of him; his mind seemed to be somewhere else as he questioned Jonas. Did he already know the answers, Jonas wondered?

"I don't know. I flew to Bombay last Saturday night, and learned Monday . . . this morning . . . from Damrong, my assistant, what had happened."

"While we are working on this problem, Mr. Adams, you might discuss it with your assistant." His voice was questioning, his manner probing as he watched for a reaction, searching the depth of Jonas' knowledge.

Jonas looked at him curiously, then stood and began pacing the floor. "I wish I could, but I haven't been able to locate him." He turned suddenly, sensing that the Prince knew Damrong's whereabouts, and he was puzzled. "Do you know where he is?" he asked, resisting the temptation to demand information.

"No," the Prince replied thoughtfully, considering the request carefully, but not willing to admit he knew anything. "Perhaps, it would be best if you waited at home for him to contact you."

"That's impossible—my telephone line has been cut."

"Most unfortunate. I am sure that can be remedied soon," the Prince replied calmly.

"But we must do something now!" Jonas turned to stare out of the window down at the city traffic, the noise faintly penetrating the second-story room in which he stood. Where, in all that mass of humanity, would he find the Thurstons? He had no idea where he should start.

"I'm sure Damrong has information," he said thoughtfully. "Where do you suggest I look for him?" He couldn't shake the feeling that the Prince was deliberately withholding information, playing a cat-and-mouse game with him.

The Prince stood up, meticulously straightened his jacket, and walked to the window to reason with the American. He respected Jonas, appreciated his business talents and his deep concern for the Thai people; but he could not, under any circumstances, give him what he wanted. He knew what Damrong was involved in, but not his location; and in any event, it would be devastating to the case if the two men met.

"Mr. Adams, please go home. Things have a way of

working out. What must be . . . ," he shrugged his shoulders significantly, ". . . must be."

Jonas nodded, knowing he had no choice but to accept the stoicism of the chief's attitude; he wasn't going to get much help from him. He turned away from the window to pick up his briefcase, then remembered the one sketch and pulled it out to lay on the desk.

"One more question," he said. "Do you know this man?" He pointed to the Chinese and looked up for a reaction.

The Prince snapped on a desk lamp, moved the paper into its light with one sedate finger. His eyes narrowed in surprise for a moment, but his answer was a guarded, "Perhaps."

"Who is he?"

The Prince didn't respond, but sat down behind the desk again, studying the different poses on the page. His cigarette lay, forgotten, in an ashtray on the desk, a trail of smoke going straight up into the air.

"I'm not going without an answer," Jonas said respectfully.

The Prince acknowledged his determination with a slight nod.

"It may be a lengthy search, and I may stir up more trouble than you need at the moment—but I'm going to find out who that man is." Previous to this moment, Jonas hadn't been particularly concerned about the man Elizabeth had sketched, but the reaction—or rather, lack of reaction—he had just received from the Prince had sharpened his curiosity. "Do you know him?"

Reluctantly, but knowing it was useless to withhold the information, the Prince answered, "Perhaps it is the present owner of Wong Exports. Why do you ask?"

Jonas ignored the question. "Wong Exports?" he repeated, trying to fit the pieces together. He didn't remember ever having any business dealings with that company. What would Wong want with him?

"Where did you get the drawings?" the Prince asked.

Jonas didn't speak immediately as he weighed the wisdom of his answer. It was his turn to hesitate about sharing information. Finally he said, "If this man has abducted them and then discovers they left evidence behind, he'll kill them without hesitation."

Prince Chandruang tried again; he had infinite patience. "Did the girl do these sketches?"

Jonas had no choice but to share what he knew. Besides, he had a feeling the Prince was way ahead of him, anyway. "Yes, she did."

"And you have not received any ransom note?"

"No," Jonas replied, startled as he took in the implications of that fact. "It hadn't occurred to me."

This confirmed the Prince's conviction that the Americans were being held for something bigger than money, and he asked, pointing to a figure on the paper, "What about that boatman? Do you know him?"

Suddenly Jonas remembered something and said in surprise, "He must have been the boatman Martin and Damrong had at the floating markets on Saturday. I saw Elizabeth sketch him, but didn't take a close look at either the man or her work. I wonder . . ." He glanced up at the Prince. "I wonder if he's the same man," he mused, indicating the other poses on the page with a tap of his finger.

Prince Chandruang's eyes grew darker, but his face was shuttered and withdrawn, even in the brightness of the lamplight. "Damrong was in his boat?" The question came quietly, but Jonas thought he sensed a slight tension behind it.

"Yes, and they talked together after the trip was over."

Jonas reached for the sketch and looked at the Prince who was staring at the desk with a pensive look—waiting for the conclusion he knew Jonas would soon make.

"Prince Chandruang," Jonas said as he slowly dropped the sketch back into his briefcase, "what's going on? What do you know about Damrong and the kidnapping? What do you know about Wong Exports?"

The Prince shook his head. "Please, Mr. Adams, go home. We will take the responsibility of finding your friends."

Jonas frowned, then his eyes narrowed as he tried to reason things out. "Sir, the man who is threatening me— could be the kidnapper. Right?"

The Prince shifted his position and pushed the writing pad into a better place on the desk, his face hardly creased with a slight smile. "Perhaps."

"It's more complicated then you're telling me," Jonas said, stating a fact rather than a question. "I'm sorry, but I just can't go home. I must do something!"

"But you know the danger of snooping around—especially as a foreigner—in some of our city's . . . unsavory areas." The Prince's voice was mild, but held a warning. He wouldn't order Jonas to go home, but would be greatly displeased to have one more westerner to keep track of during the night.

"I know," Jonas argued, "but these people are important to me."

Both men eyed one another respectfully, challengingly, in the silent room. Finally, the Prince shrugged his shoulders slightly and smiled at Jonas. "What will be . . . ," he repeated, ". . . will be."

Jonas nodded and stepped back from the desk. He put his hands together chest high in the traditional Thai greeting, and bowed slightly to the Prince. "I'm grateful for so much of your time tonight; I know you're a busy man. Good night, Sir."

When the Prince was alone, he made a telephone call to

someone on an extension number. A few minutes later, Jonas saw two Thai policemen get into a jeep and follow him as he drove away from the building.

There was no value in trying to contact Damrong, Jonas thought as he negotiated the traffic, for the Prince had hinted strongly that he wouldn't be successful, but Jonas would give the contents of his bank account to know where his assistant was and what he was doing.

He knew Damrong had discussed the business situation with the police several times lately, but things just weren't adding up right; there was a discordant note in his mind as he tried to make plans for his search.

Perhaps the best move was to get into the Thurston's hotel room to see what he might find. As he took the smaller, less traveled streets, and even an alley, he saw the jeep following him and figured the Prince planned to keep well informed on his activities. He couldn't do anything about that, but what would he do if they tried to prevent him from some action he thought necessary?

As he drove into the hotel driveway he was faced with the reality of getting into the rooms. He was sure the manager wouldn't give him a key and there were bars at the windows. Well, he had never picked a lock in his life, but he wouldn't learn any younger, he thought grimly.

He parked the car in the shadows as near to the side entrance as possible, and not wanting to be seen, cut across the edge of the lawn, mounted the veranda quickly and entered the side door as quietly as he could.

Just as he got to Elizabeth's room he heard voices inside and stepped closer to the door to listen.

"Did you get all his clothes into the suitcase?" a woman's voice asked.

There was a mumbled reply which Jonas didn't catch.

He heard someone opening and closing drawers hurriedly, then that same voice again.

"I've got all her things. Come on, we'd better get out of here."

The voices were getting louder and closer and, for a second, Jonas toyed with the idea of entering the room to confront the thieves. He was furious, knowing that someone was stealing the Thurston's belongings. Then logic took over, and he knew it would be better to follow as they left the room, just in case they would lead him to the his friends.

He ducked into a small pantry beside Elizabeth's room just as the door opened and the two Americans that Elizabeth had sketched walked out into the hallway, carrying luggage that belonged to the Thurstons. He recognized the pieces that he had carried for Elizabeth.

They, too, had no interest in being observed, and were so intent upon getting out of the hotel unnoticed that they didn't see Jonas watching them. They made their way to the side exit; Jonas was down the hall and after them as soon as they had gone outside. On the veranda, he waited until they were out at the edge of the lawn before he ducked down along the railing and ran toward his car. It was fortunate that they were parked closer to the street and were only getting into a car by the time Jonas was in his and had the motor running.

He concentrated on keeping them in sight, and for once, wished his own car was not white; it stood out in the darkness and made it impossible to be overlooked.

Glancing in the rear view mirror, he saw the police behind him, and frowned in irritation, hoping no one noticed three cars proceeding through the city like a parade. He kept about a half a block behind the Americans, and as they headed toward the Chinese district, wondered about the possibility of Wong owning a warehouse in that area—it would be logical. And what were the Americans doing with that luggage? Were they stealing it for themselves or delivering it to the Thurstons?

When they turned into an alley, he pulled over to the curb, jumped out and sprinted forward, not wanting to lose sight of their car. Since it was the only one in the alley, he had to follow on foot. He saw the tail lights disappear around a corner and kept running, dodging several Chinese men out for a late night stroll, and a lot of trash and garbage, wondering if the police were behind him.

Around the third corner, the car pulled up in front of a warehouse and the Americans got out and followed the Chinese driver into the building. The door they entered wasn't locked or guarded; Jonas wondered if the Thurstons were there. He would have a look around to be sure.

Keeping in the shadows, he began a search around the building, walking carefully to avoid loose stones or debris that might give his presence away. There wasn't much light close to the warehouse, except that which fell from a room on the second story, so he didn't know what to expect.

He was about to try a door at the back of the building when it was suddenly flung open, flattening him back against the wall; he was hardly breathing in an effort not to be seen. An old Chinese grandmother shuffled out, following the feeble light that spilled timidly out into the yard.

She carried a pail full of garbage, which she threw into the river with the same vigor that she talked—vociferously arguing with someone inside the room. As she turned to walk back to the building, Jonas waited to be discovered, visions of an ominous situation racing through his mind. But, he wasn't a television detective who could fast-talk his way out of such difficulties; so he waited, feeling extremely foolish and even more endangered.

But the old woman's eyes were on the uneven ground, her steps faltering in the dim light, and her mouth going like an oriental recording. She failed to see Jonas standing in the shadows.

This must be the living quarters of the resident night watchman, who was at the moment being out-talked by his wife. Jonas thought of questioning them, but then assumed they would only alert the owners. When the door slammed shut, he breathed deeply and let the air go slowly from his lungs as he slumped against the wall for a long minute.

Then he moved on, looking for any other opening in the warehouse, so that he could search for the Thurstons. Rounding the far end of the building, he saw another entrance, and on closer inspection, realized that it had been recently smashed and the barricade was inadequate— probably a permanent solution was to be made in the morning. He felt over the boards that were nailed across the door—there was just enough room for him to squeeze through. Taking a quick look in both directions as he thought of the police shadowing him somewhere in the darkness, he ducked down and wiggled through, tearing his shirt sleeve in his effort to get in.

It didn't make sense to have left this back door so open and unguarded if the Thurstons were around, but he had to find out if they were and why their luggage had been brought in.

Reaching out, he felt along the wall, and touched a handrail slanting upward—a stairway. He lifted a foot and tested the first step gingerly. With deliberate meticulousness, he tested each step to be sure it would hold his weight. At the top, he slowly pulled a door open and found himself in a long, dimly-lit corridor. Just as he went through, he glanced back down the stairs to see another figure crawling through the space he had used. It could be one of the policemen following him or someone guarding the warehouse; he wasn't going to wait to find out. He pulled the door shut and moved silently down the hallway, checking each room as he went by.

He was halfway down the hall when he heard the back door open and he ducked into a room and waited. With a quick glance around, he could see a table, several chairs and two narrow cots.

There wasn't a sound outside the room and when a dark form finally appeared in the doorway, Jonas' heart thudded in reaction, until he realized it was the police. He reached out to grab the man's arm and found himself facing a gun. He made a mental note never to touch an armed man like that again.

"Put that away," he whispered, moving into the hall so that he might be seen.

"You should not be in here, Sir," the man said, slipping the gun back into its holster.

"I want to find out if the Thurstons are here," he argued, and continued his silent search, which led to a closed door. He turned toward the man behind him. "Who owns this warehouse?"

"Wong Exports," the man replied, speaking in his own language.

Jonas answered in Thai. "I might have known." He had the hall door open by then and could see a room at the far end. Its door was closed, but light was spilling out around the curtains at the windows. "And that?" he motioned toward the room.

"The office. I don't believe your friends are in the building, Sir."

"Why not?" Jonas whispered as he continued watching the office.

"There aren't any guards around."

Just then the office door opened and Jonas jumped back and eased the hall door shut. "Someone's coming," he whispered.

Both men ducked into a small room near the door, and heard it open. From the shadows they saw two Americans down the corridor being escorted by a tough-looking Chinese and, in a moment, heard them locked in a room. As he made his way back, the Chinese stopped at each room, turned on the light and made a quick search to be sure everything was all right.

Jonas and his companion squeezed down behind a long, empty bin and waited.

The light clicked on and footsteps came across the room. There was a hair-raising silence while Jonas wondered if they had been discovered.

The Thai eased his gun from its place on his hip and raised it up, but Jonas shook his head and put out a restraining hand. He didn't want anyone killed in his defense.

The moments seemed to drag on and on as their tension increased. What was that man doing? Had he discovered that they were there? Why wouldn't he move?

At any moment, Jonas expected to hear a gunshot and feel a bullet ripping through his body. He reminded the Lord that he wasn't a quick-witted investigator, just an ordinary human being in need of instantaneous deliverance.

He shot a quick look of relief at his companion when they heard footsteps move back across the room. The light was snapped off and they were in darkness again.

Jonas expelled his breath softly when the hall door slammed shut.

"Please, Sir," the policeman said, still crouching next to him, "let's get out of here before we are discovered."

"Will you force me?" Jonas whispered.

"If I must."

Jonas wondered if instructions had been given to keep him away from this warehouse and from its owner. Chandruang was out for big game and wouldn't let one foreigner scramble his plans; but Jonas had to wonder why there weren't more of Chandruang's men around the building.

He was determined, however, to find out what he could, and he stood up and moved cautiously out of the room, opened the hall door again, and before the policeman could stop him, went through. He felt the man's hand on his arm, but he shook it off and went on, aiming for a darkened room next to the office where he hoped to do some successful eavesdropping.

He felt his way around several boxes scattered carelessly around and was just nearing the wall when he stepped on a bottle half hidden in the dim light, and before he could bend over to stop its flight, it slammed against the wall nearest the office.

He grunted softly and whirled around to look for a hiding place, but there was nothing but a lot of small boxes stacked around. He saw his companion move behind the door and motion for him to follow.

In a second they heard the office door flung open, and a voice barking out orders in Chinese. Someone was coming to search the room and they would surely be found. Jonas knew he had really blundered this time and regretted what was about to happen to the man next to him just because he had been so determined to find the Thurstons.

But just as one of the guards stood in the doorway with his hand on the light switch, there was a loud, insistent pounding on the front door of the warehouse. They could hear someone shouting in Thai, "Open up! Immediately, open up!"

There was a rush of footsteps toward the front stairway, and a voice, angry and vicious, shouting in Thai, "One moment!"

Jonas saw three shadows descend the stairway, and pulled at his companion's arm. "Quick, let's get out of here!"

Jonas felt the hair on his neck stand on end as he made a

silent dash for the hall door; he expected to be caught at any moment. But the men from the office were still down at the front door, arguing loudly with their visitors.

As they sped down the hallway to the back door, the Thai whispered, "My partner came not a moment too soon."

Remembering that the two Americans locked in one of those rooms might hear them, Jonas didn't ask any questions until they were free of the boards at the back entrance and stood outside drinking in free air.

"Did you say that was your partner at the front door?" Jonas asked while gasping for some air.

"Yes."

"How do you know?"

"I told him to wait fifteen minutes and then create a commotion at the front door."

"Wise man," Jonas admitted thankfully.

They moved into the bushes along the riverbank as they rounded the side of the warehouse where they could watch what was happening at the front door.

Three men in uniform stood talking to someone inside; Jonas wished he could see who it was.

As they stood, waiting and watching in the darkness, Jonas felt the mass of humanity in the crowded Chinese district. People tended to spend much of their lives out of doors in the tropics, and long after they had shuttered their doors and windows against the evil spirits, the night still throbbed with the residue of the day's activities. Only a feeble glimmer here and there, a voice calling out, a clanging beat of distant music—only these were physical confirmations that there was still life in the darkened buildings that surrounded the warehouse.

He heard someone say "good-night" rather sharply and watched the door close effectively on the police, who then moved off toward the alley.

"Your friends are not in that building," his companion said in a low voice.

"You're sure?"

"Yes."

"Where are they?"

"I am sorry, Sir. I do not know."

Jonas sighed, feeling defeated even as the precise pronunciation of the Thai's English registered on his mind, as it always did. He enjoyed hearing the local people speak his native language; they often had better command of English than most Americans did.

"And if you knew where they were, you wouldn't tell me. Right?"

The man nodded.

The front door of the warehouse opened again, and Jonas looked up to see two men exit and get into the black car. The motor sprang to life and the driver turned the car around before going back down the alley toward the main street.

"Wong," the policeman said briefly.

"You're sure?"

"Yes," and in answer to Jonas' thoughts, said, "he usually goes home this time of night."

"I'm going to see if he does," Jonas replied and started to run after the car, the two policemen joining him.

"Where does he live?" he asked as they neared his own car on the street.

Neither of the men answered. Either they didn't know, or else they had been instructed to be as uninformative as possible.

Jonas opened his car door and got in, pushed the key into the ignition and gave it a twist—but the motor refused to turn over. He groaned and tried several times, all the while watching Wong's car move further down the street.

"May I help you?" His police friend leaned over to talk

to him through the window.

Jonas glanced up. "Put back whatever it was you took out," he said and pulled back the hood release.

"I will see if I can do anything for you, Sir." The young man refused to be drawn into Jonas' implication that they had tampered with his car, and moved around to raise the hood. In a moment, he stepped back into Jonas' vision and suggested he try again.

Jonas turned the key and the motor began to purr. It was futile for him to get angry; Wong's car had disappeared, and the young man had merely been doing his job. But he couldn't resist one jab.

After thanking the man for his help, Jonas said, "In case you lose me in traffic, I'm going to my office."

Seven

When Elizabeth came to—her brain dizzy and unbalanced, her senses rejecting something sinister that loomed in the darkness—Martin was in the boat, supporting her in his arms. It took a moment for her to remember where she was and what had caused her to black out. Then, the fear of imminent death, the heartbreak of Damrong's betrayal, the physical pain caused by the fever she had, washed over her mind and she choked back a sob.

Damrong was still there, but his attention was focused on someone on the pier; it was Wong, and one of the two men with him held the spotlight that had moments before illuminated their escape attempt. The light was dimmer now—they didn't want to attract attention—but she knew without looking that one of those men held a gun on them.

"Well," Wong said in a harsh tone, "since you seem to enjoy boat rides so much, we'll let you have one now."

Elizabeth stiffened in fear and tried to sit up, afraid that he meant to send them to their death in that dark river; but he went on, "Damrong, you and Chen take them to the

Nakornmai Temple. Tie them up and stay with them until I get there."

Damrong jerked his head up at this order. "Go with them? Why? I've got to get back to Jonas Adams before he becomes suspicious!"

"No. That's precisely what you won't do—get to Adams. How do I know you aren't deceiving me? You'll stay where I can keep an eye on you. And, Damrong—if you're trying to frame me . . ." Wong stopped, leaving his threat hanging in mid-air, watching Damrong through the timid glow of the spotlight.

"That would be very foolish of me, wouldn't it," Damrong said quietly.

Wong grunted in agreement. "It would indeed."

"You told me to get one of Adams' shipments ready. I still need to do that if you want things to go off as planned tomorrow. I haven't planted the . . ."

Wong interrupted him angrily. *"We'll* take care of that!" He took a step closer to the boat and stared down at Damrong. "If you can't follow orders, I'll have you re-placed right now!" he threatened, drawing out of his pocket that same evil-looking knife he had played with so lovingly in his office.

Damrong returned the look without flinching, though he understood the message—Wong would kill him on the spot if he caused trouble. "I told you I would help you get rid of Adams—I meant it."

They were speaking English—for the prisoners' bene-fit—and Elizabeth gasped, then felt Martin's arm tighten around her shoulder warningly. In Wong's present mood, any response from them might trigger that streak of warped maliciousness he had already displayed. The best they could do now was to keep quiet and hope for another opportunity to try to escape.

"Do you have your keys with you?" Wong asked

Damrong, holding out his hand and barely controlling his animosity.

"What keys?" Damrong's expression was one of genuine innocence, but it irritated Wong.

"For the Adams warehouse, you stupid . . .!"

Damrong's lips stiffened, but he silently dug into his pocket and pulled out a set of keys which he handed to Wong.

The look on Wong's face was as dangerous as that of a cobra Elizabeth had once seen, and she shivered with raw, cold fear. He smiled coldly at Damrong. "I hope, for your family's sake, that you aren't playing games with me." He paused significantly, and then added, "Now, get those two away from here. If the police are hunting for two foreigners, all of these warehouses along here will be searched. They won't ever think of that old, abandoned temple."

Damrong nodded, turned and spoke to the boatman in Thai, instructing him to pole away from the pier before starting the engine.

Elizabeth listened to this exchange with a heavy heart and turned her face into Martin's shoulder for comfort. She just couldn't believe Damrong was betraying Jonas. How could he? He had been a friend of Jonas for many years, and he was regarded as more than just a manager of a business; she had seen the affection Jonas had for him. And what would he gain in such an association with Wong? It was obvious that his position with the Chinese was dangerously precarious; his life wasn't worth an American penny. Wong would take as much delight in killing Damrong as he would in destroying that harmless household lizard that was so prevalent in the tropics. No, Elizabeth just couldn't fathom Damrong's reasoning. He must be mad!

Damrong took the gun from Chen's hand and sat down. He turned to Martin and spoke, his voice barely audible.

"We won't tie you up or gag you, but, Martin, don't try anything. I'll use this," he waved the gun slightly, "if I have to."

Chen leaned over and said something to Damrong, who nodded and spoke again. "Not a word from either of you while we're in the boat. Voices carry easily over the water."

Silently they watched Chen start the motor and turn the boat upstream. They moved past darkened warehouses, saw modern hotels lit up like giant chandeliers, and passed several temples Elizabeth couldn't identify. When they moved under the Thonburi bridge, she looked up, hoping for that slight chance that someone might be driving by and look down—but the traffic was moving too quickly. There were hundreds of people—Thai and Chinese—who populated the river's edge in one way or another, and, occasionally she saw dark forms moving along in the night—but Chen kept the boat far enough away from the river bank to prevent anyone seeing who the passengers were, should anyone just happen to have the slightest interest. Most of them, she thought gloomily, wisely ignored what went on in the dark; it was never healthy to know too much.

Not wanting to ram some unseen craft in the darkness, Chen kept the motor low, and the slow *putt-putt* sound was swallowed up with other city noises. In a few minutes they were passing the five-towered Temple of Dawn on the west and the Grand Palace on the east with its royal grounds where the Temple of the Emerald Buddha stood. In other circumstances, it would have been an impressive sight at night, but now it left Elizabeth cold.

All of it represented a religion that mockingly challenged her belief that Jesus Christ was the only God, who had come to meet with man, had even gone so far as to be sacrificed on a cross for man. But, Elizabeth tried to reassure her tired and confused mind. He was *not* a dead god whose image was plastered with gold leaf and who stared with unseeing eyes from an impassioned face, kept in temples where there was no joy nor communication between god and man. Jesus had come to give life—eternal life—and her present difficulties didn't change that fact.

Her faith in God could remain as constant in the face of death, if she so chose, as it was in the comfortable, tranquil days of her life. God had not changed, nor fallen asleep; He was not hiding behind clouds, cowering in an inability to help His creation.

She supposed that the problem came when she tried to tell God what to do, how to answer her prayers, and then became angry and fearful with Him when He chose to work in other ways.

It started to rain again, and Damrong motioned for them to move in under the canvas cover. "You don't need to get soaked yet," he said. "It will be wet enough where you're going, I'm afraid."

When the boat finally pulled into shore, the city had been left behind, and crowding close to the water was a large, black, cone-like silhouette of the temple hovering over them like one of those monsters from children's nightmares.

There was just a light sprinkle of rain as Chen tied up to a wooden pier and Damrong motioned the Thurstons out of the boat.

"Where are we?" Elizabeth asked, wondering if there wasn't a small village close by where they might find a rescuer.

"This temple was abandoned years ago," Damrong said, as he stepped out of the boat. "The government hasn't refurbished it, and no one comes to worship here any more. The walls are crumbling—the whole temple could fall at any moment.".

He was hardly reassuring, Elizabeth thought, as she

stood staring at the scene around them. There was no one nearby, she could sense that. Humanity had been left behind in the city; here they were the only four people within miles. It was a desolate feeling, just as though they were being forced into a tiny, black, forgotten hole in the earth, from which they would never emerge. She shivered with fever and apprehension, hardly noticing the rain nor cool night air.

The pier led straight to an entrance into the temple. Monks of former times must have made it a practice to arrive by boat, but lack of use for years had led to the present deterioration.

"Careful," Damrong warned, "the wood is rotted through in many places." Even so, he motioned for them to move forward.

Seeing Chen's hesitation to follow, Damrong turned to urge him on. There was a short discussion between them in the drizzling rain and then Damrong grunted in disgust and by threatening with the gun, forced Chen down the landing.

"What's the matter?" Martin asked, his arm around Elizabeth, guiding her slowly over a broken place in the wood planks.

"He's afraid of the ghosts," Damrong answered. "And of the snakes and scorpions."

"I wish you hadn't said that," Elizabeth breathed apprehensively, and stopped walking. "Please," she begged, "do we have to go in there?"

Damrong was insistent. "Wong ordered you into this temple, and that's where you're going."

He turned his flashlight on and directed the beam up the side of the temple. The stones had a moldy green color, and many were missing. The top half of the thin spire was broken off. The entrance nearest them had no protective door, but was built so that very little of the interior could be seen from the river. Damrong flashed the light over the ground surrounding the temple; it was completely covered with flood water and its depth was difficult to assess, but it looked as though the temple had been built *in* the river, not beside it. The entire picture was not one of a safe refuge.

"The fields are covered with water now, so there won't be any farmers out; no one to hear your cries for help." Damrong's voice was stoic, and he directed the light toward the entrance again.

"Inside," he instructed Chen, and then threw the light onto the pier in order to guide Elizabeth and Martin into the building.

Elizabeth could see nothing else of the interior of the temple other than the small room where they were to be kept. For the moment, that was dreary enough.

The walls were made of stone and glistened with moisture, throwing out a heavy, damp coldness that enveloped anyone who dared enter the room. There was a stone platform about three feet high that ran around all sides of the room—religious relics would have been kept there—and it was divided on each side by a metal rod embedded high up in the wall with the other end sunk into the edge of the platform.

Chen produced a rope from the boat and tied their hands to either side of a rod, so that they both could lie down on the platform to sleep.

But Elizabeth's flesh crawled at the thought of stretching out to sleep; she was afraid of the snakes and scorpions. Shaking violently from fever and chilled to the bone, she had another thought. "Damrong," she asked, "will the temple be flooded?"

His answer was not reassuring. "Some years, when the floods are high enough, it does."

The two men sat on the ledge, on either side of the doorway, and when Damrong snapped his flashlight off, Chen began to complain, a stream of Chinese filling the air. A flashlight snapped on, and Elizabeth saw that it was Chen's. Apparently, he wasn't planning to sit in the dark for the rest of the night; he wanted to see danger before it struck.

He flashed the light nervously around the floor, looking for those creatures he dreaded. Passing around the ledge and up some of the wall, hesitating around stones that jutted out and provided hiding places, the light rested on an inner doorway and flashed out into another room.

Elizabeth caught her breath. "Oh, please, Damrong," she begged again, "please take us out of here. Can't you see that room is already flooded? Martin, make him take us out of here!" Her voice broke on a sob, and she leaned over against Martin's shoulder, a wave of uncontrollable shivering going through her.

"Easy, Liz. We'll be all right," he said, trying to comfort her. "Calm down, Liz. The Lord is with us; He won't forsake us." His voice was affirming and he talked on, reminding her of God's love and care.

"Turn that light off," Damrong ordered Chen, who couldn't seem to stop staring into that flooded area. But the light dropped down to the edge of the doorway; Chen wasn't too sure that some snake wasn't going to come crawling out of the water.

"Try not to worry, Miss Thurston," Damrong said stiffly. "That room is much lower than this one. We are in no danger now." If he meant to be encouraging he failed, for his voice lacked the warmth that had always been there.

"What is the matter with you?" Elizabeth demanded of Damrong, her voice shaking now with anger. "How can you do this to us? How can you even think of harming Jonas!"

"You don't understand," Damrong mumbled.

Chen's light flashed back and forth as the two talked; resting first on Elizabeth's face as she threw out her accusations, and then on Damrong as he answered. "What is wrong?'' he asked Damrong, speaking again in Thai, for that was the only language they shared.

''Be quiet!'' Damrong growled. ''Let her talk!''

Elizabeth couldn't stop talking, for her fear and apprehensions had found a place of release as she lashed out at this injustice.

''Jonas is a good man; just remember the way he's helped your own people! He's given so much, cared so much; and all the time you've been like a . . . a snake waiting to strike out at him.'' She remembered some of the things Martin had told her. ''Jonas has used his own plane to fly people to hospitals, gone into flooded areas to rescue others, made you a manager of his firm. He's willing to give everything he has for Thailand, but you want to take his life! And you call yourself a Christian! You can't have God's love in your heart and be involved in such a traitorous act! You just can't!''

''Easy, Liz,'' Martin said quietly. ''We'll be all right.'' He had to break her tirade before she got hysterical. ''Maybe we don't know the whole story yet. Let's just wait to see what takes place.''

''I'm so cold,'' she whimpered and dropped her weary head against his shoulder, ignoring Damrong's attempt to defend himself.

''Is there anything in the boat that Elizabeth can use for a covering?'' Martin asked, directing his question at Damrong. ''She's going to catch pneumonia in here.''

Chen was sent to the boat and returned shortly with a strip of canvas and an old sweater someone had left behind. He spread the canvas out on the ledge to break the dampness where the Thurstons were sitting. When Damrong gently tried to put the sweater around Elizabeth's shoulders, she knocked his hand away.

''Don't touch me,'' she said, gritting her teeth.

Without a word of reproof, he handed the sweater to

Chen and watched as it was flung carelessly around her shoulders, then returned to his place across the room.

"What time is it, Martin?" Elizabeth dropped her head on his arm again. "I feel as though it should be morning."

"It's just a little past midnight," he replied, after having checked the glow of his watch. "Try to get some sleep, Liz."

"Do you think Wong plans to leave us here to drown or be bitten by a poisonous snake?"

"Hush, Liz. It doesn't help to think about all the possibilities. God knows what will happen; we are in His hands."

"Oh, Martin, I don't want to die without seeing Mom and Dad again. And they don't even know we're here in Thailand!"

"Don't think about it now. Things will look better in the morning."

"But suppose the river rises?"

Martin laughed ruefully. "I don't think Chen is going to let it happen without us knowing about it. Unless the batteries in his flashlight die."

"Martin," Elizabeth said, unable to let go of her worries, "no one in this world knows we're here! We're all alone!"

She heard a moan from one of the men across the room. Surely it wasn't Damrong feeling sympathetic for them. Why should he care what she said or felt, if he was so intent upon helping Wong in his evil plans. He was committed to harming Jonas; she couldn't believe that her plight would be of the slightest concern to him. Perhaps he had dropped off to sleep, and her talking had disturbed him. She hoped that was the case; he deserved to be bothered.

"We're not alone, Liz. Jesus promised that He would be with us always."

"I know, I know," she said softly. "It's just so difficult to control my thoughts. I wouldn't be so afraid if I could just keep my mind on Christ. But, Martin, I keep thinking that perhaps it is in God's plan for us to die here, and I don't want to face that. When I think that He may not want to deliver us from this, I just panic."

"I don't know the future, Liz, but I do know that our times are in His hands. Right now, at this very moment, we are protected. We can rest in that, and leave tomorrow to Him."

It was a long, terrifying, nerve-ripping, never-ending night. Elizabeth knew she was not alone in such an experience, for every person has had a personal crucible. Call it a night of horror or pain or human suffering; call it what you will, she thought wearily, all such nights had one thing in common—it tries the soul to the limit—and beyond.

She went through many emotions—there was searing anger at Damrong, stomach-churning fear of Wong, quiet peace as God's Word flowed into her mind, confusion as the darkness and weariness pulled at her, even acceptance as the fever sapped her strength.

Scenes flashed through her mind—some torture they were yet to endure, a snake crawling over her, dying in the dark river waters—and she turned hot all over and began to perspire. Then she tried to pray and quote scriptures aloud, seeking to dispell her fears.

"I will both lay me down in peace and sleep, for Thou Lord, only makest me to dwell in safety." She mumbled part of the words aloud, and the rest simply ran through her tired mind.

And a phrase so popular in the Psalms kept repeating itself over and over—"The Lord reigns . . . the Lord reigns . . . the Lord . . . reigns."

She tried to sleep, and did succeed in dozing off a few

times; but when she jerked back into full consciousness, she would turn to ask Martin the time.

"Won't morning ever come!" she complained when being told it was just three o'clock in the morning.

"Only a couple more hours, and it should begin to get light," Martin said encouragingly.

"Then what will happen?" she murmured. "Wong will come then, won't he?" She started to stretch her legs out on the ledge, then thought better of it when she remembered the possibility of scorpions—their bites were extremely painful. "I wonder where Jonas is?"

"In town." Damrong's reply came softly, and unexpectedly, in the darkness.

"How do you know?" she asked, still unable to show the slightest regard for the Thai's feelings, still wanting to make him suffer.

"I talked with him this morning . . . no, I mean yesterday morning. He was in Bombay, but when he heard that you had been kidnapped, he said he would fly home immediately. I don't think there would be much that would detain him; he was very concerned . . . about you." His voice trailed off, perhaps realizing the futility of encouraging her, perhaps embarrassed.

"And you let him come!" she accused harshly. "You knew what was going to happen. Why didn't you tell him to stay there?"

Damrong laughed regretfully. "You don't think he would listen to me, do you? He was determined to return to Bangkok. I'm not his boss."

"And you aren't his friend, either!"

There was no reply, and since Elizabeth could barely see across the room because of the weakening flashlight, she couldn't tell what Damrong's reaction was to her accusations.

Chen was amused that she was angry; every time she

lashed out, he chuckled and made some remark, and Elizabeth was surprised that Damrong took it all without annoyance. She had expected that he would defend himself, but he didn't—he just listened, answered when he could, and let the rest go. His oriental mind must be rejecting her anger as merely feminine outbursts, or he might be waiting for the most opportune moment for revenge.

Finally, around four o'clock, Chen's light slowly faded away. Elizabeth edged as close to Martin as she could, and felt her skin crawl in anticipation.

"The snakes won't necessarily come now just because that feeble light is gone," Martin said kindly.

She acknowledged this bit of wisdom with a small laugh, laid her head back against the wall and closed her eyes. The fever didn't seem as high as earlier in the night, and she was thankful for that.

"Liz," Martin called softly.

"Hm?"

"Why don't you try to sleep? You've been quite restless all night."

"I'm sorry, Martin, if I kept you from sleeping."

"You know I don't mind. How is the fever—still high?"

"No, I don't think so." She was quiet for a moment; her next words surprising Martin. "I wonder what Peter is doing now?" Her voice lacked its usual harshness when she spoke of her former fiance.

"Ready to give up your resentment, Liz?"

"I . . . I don't know."

"You'll have to deal with it sooner or later, Liz. You don't want to spend the rest of your life letting that eat away at you, do you?"

"The rest of my life may only be a few more hours," she said sadly.

"No, we're going to get out of this mess," Martin replied with such assurance that Liz turned to him in surprise.

"Do you really believe that?"

"Of course, I do. I'm firmly convinced that the Lord is going to deliver us. But, what about your problem with Peter?" Martin was persistent, and while Elizabeth resented being forced to face the subject again, she also was a little relieved. She was tired of fighting, tired of being angry. Deep inside she wanted to make things right.

Something she had said to Damrong earlier popped into her mind—'You can't be a Christian and do this to Jonas! You just can't!'

Should that same judgment be brought upon her own life? The grudge she held toward Peter certainly wasn't Christian.

"I remember Jonas telling me about someone he knew whose life was ruined because of bitterness. He's right, I know it; but, Martin, it's so hard to let go!"

"Do you remember Uncle Stacy?"

"Yes, how could I forget him? He used to terrify me when we were in the States on furlough. That stern, unhappy face and sharp, dictatorial voice. He was a miserable man."

Martin shifted his position—the stone ledge was getting extremely hard and uncomfortable. "I remember hearing Mom and Dad talk about him, trying to help us understand. He was hurt deeply by his parents when he was a child, and all his life, he mistrusted the actions of others."

"Did you ever find out what they did to him?"

"No. Mom told me once that he would never discuss it. But he sure liked to criticize the human frailties of others. He felt everyone was taking advantage of him; no one could do anything right. But, Liz, he was a lonely, miserable man! You don't want to end up like that."

Elizabeth didn't respond. That wasn't what she wanted to be, but it was so hard to let go, to tell the Lord that it didn't matter if someone had been cruel to her. To give up personal rights—the advantages every human being feels are theirs—was so difficult. She had years ago given up her right to an easier life in the United States, for she wanted to share God's love with others. She had even given up her right to a happy, normal family life when she was old enough to understand, even though she cried at night for her parents. She had understood that sacrifice was on behalf of others. She was willing to be mocked by non-believers—that wasn't important.

She went on, silently telling the Lord all that she had given up because she loved Him. The right to physical comforts, the right to the stability of life-long friends nearby, the right to many other choices. But, she couldn't erase from her mind the one right that she was clutching like a lifeline—the right not to be crushed by someone she had loved. To tell the Lord that she willingly accepted this blow, would not fight it, would not hold resentment, would not hate—she just didn't think she could do it.

"It isn't worth it, Liz." Martin's soft warning startled her, as it dug straight into her jumbled thoughts.

"I know."

"The first step is the hardest; but you need to say that you are willing to forgive." Martin was pushing a little, trying to help her resolve this difficulty.

She stared into the darkness, aware that there were shapes forming in the room as the time drew nearer sunrise. Dawn was coming, silently but surely. She admitted a mute awareness of her need to be rid of the bitterness she had carried the last few months, and slowly, silently, like the dawn, there grew an honest desire to get everything right.

Silently, even reluctantly, she prayed, confessing the sin of bitterness and her satisfaction in letting it grow in her life. She admitted that she no longer wanted any part of it. The words "I forgive" were so hard to form, even in her mind, but she did it anyway, knowing it was the only way toward peace.

"I don't want it any more," she said, unaware that she had whispered aloud.

"Want what?" Martin asked.

Her eyes flew open and she could see Martin watching her—his face lined with fatigue but still serene—and she smiled. "I don't want to be bitter any more."

"Good for you. Can you forgive Peter?"

She took a deep breath and then sighed. "Yes, I think so. It still hurts, but, yes, I forgive him."

"Why?"

"Well, it doesn't have anything to do with what happens to us now, I'm just tired of carrying that around. I don't want anything in my life that will separate me from Christ's presence and love—it isn't worth it."

And finally, for the first time in weeks, she felt free of the bitterness that had taken root unawares and almost smothered out her spiritual life. "Lord, forgive me," she whispered.

"And forgive yourself, too, Liz."

Yes, that, too, she thought. To allow God to work freely in her life, she had to accept His forgiveness. Otherwise, she would never feel worthy of serving Him.

"If we get out of this, Martin, I'm going to write to Peter. I need to let him know that what happened is OK." A tear trickled down her cheek, and she took a deep breath to hold back the tears waiting to be shed. She glanced at Damrong as she talked and was surprised when he looked at her with what she could only regard as approval. Then, standing up abruptly, he walked over to check the room that was flooded.

"Well, what's wrong with him?" she asked.

"I don't know . . . yet," Martin replied, his voice barely audible. "I think there are some strange things going on in his mind. I just wish I could get a chance to talk to him without Chen around.'' He leaned over and called softly, ''Damrong?''

Reluctantly, he turned and walked over to stand in front of them, uncomfortably ignoring Elizabeth while he listened to Martin's request.

''Untie me, Damrong; let me walk out on the pier for a minute. You could go with me. I won't try anything.''

Damrong looked down at Martin's hands, pushed the ropes aside and saw the raw spots around his wrists. ''You tried to get loose last night?''

Martin smiled slightly and shrugged his shoulders. ''The ropes were too tight. You can't blame me, can you?''

Damrong didn't answer, but stood, thoughtfully searching Martin's face. ''All right,'' he said reluctantly, ''I'll let you walk for a minute.'' He reached out to untie the ropes.

A sound from the river halted his actions, and he turned quickly and went to look through the outer door.

''There's a boat coming.''

''Can you tell who it is?'' Martin asked.

''No, not yet, but it's coming in to shore. Chen, wake up. We have company.''

But who, Elizabeth wondered, her stomach knotting up in fear again.

Eight

Jonas glanced out the car window at the now-empty street, threw the gear into drive, and pulled quickly away from the curb, his irritation at being thwarted by the police needling him into unusual recklessness. His movements were entirely automatic, all done without thought—braking for lights, turning at correct corners, dodging careless pedestrians.

By the time he pulled into a parking place next to the building, his anger was directed inward at his incompetence. He jerked the keys from the ignition and then, in frustration, folded his arms over the steering wheel and sat staring at the neon sign that read *Adams Export Ltd*. It was a visible indication of five years of successful labor, but he knew that little in that time had prepared him for the present intrigue. He wasn't making any progress in finding the Thurstons, and all he could now do was try to locate a man named Wong; although, what he would do or say, should he succeed, he didn't know. He felt as though his efforts had been as successful as throwing pebbles at the moon, and it was frightening because the longer the Thurstons were held captive, the greater their danger.

Reaching into the back seat, he picked up his briefcase and turned to get out of the car. The glare of lights in the rear view mirror caught his attention and he frowningly watched a police jeep pull up to the curb at the next corner. Probably the same two men who had followed him to the warehouse, he thought with irritation as he got out, locked the car, and made his way into the building for the second time that night.

As he flicked on the lights, he could see from the front window that the police weren't going anywhere, evidently content to wait there for his next move. And what would that be he wondered as he ambled slowly around the room, looking for anything that might lead to some positive action.

Should he try to locate Wong's home? Pastor Chu, from the largest Chinese church in the city, would probably have the information he needed, but it was past midnight and Jonas couldn't disturb him now. Perhaps he would visit the pastor after breakfast.

He stopped at Joy's desk, picked up the telephone book and flipped through the pages to the "W" section, acknowledging as he did so that there would be too many Wongs and he wouldn't find what he needed. He knew a number of men by that name, but none were exporters; and he wondered why he had never met this one, particularly since they were in the same business. Wong, or one of his subordinates, had probably dealt with Damrong.

Jonas continued to pace around the room, stopping at a display table to shift an intricately carved, teakwood elephant sitting on a glass pedestal, run a finger lightly over an expensive and delicately shaped silver necklace, and move other items around in an attempt to hang on to reality.

Even as he contemplated finding Wong, he had to admit that Prince Chandruang would prevent any contact, especially if Wong was really the Red Tiger. The Red Tiger, he thought grimly; the man accused of the most atrocious deeds, ready to kill at a whim, amused at the sufferings of others—this man could be holding the Thurstons!

He wondered if the police had control of the situation. Were they aware of the Red Tiger's operations, and did they have plans to catch him? Or were they simply content to let the Asian gangster pursue his underworld activities as long as he didn't harm them or interfere with their personal ambitions? And even more pertinent—could the Prince be trusted if Jonas got into trouble trying to find the Thurstons? He didn't mean to cast doubts upon the Prince's integrity, but he was worried.

"I don't know," Jonas muttered as he leaned dejectedly against the door frame of Damrong's office. "Damrong, wherever you are, get to a telephone and call me!" The irritation in his plea wasn't directed toward his assistant, but toward his own helplessness. He looked over the desk top, wondering if Damrong had left some information, and noticed a paper next to the telephone that was full of scribbling. Jonas frowned and leaned over for a closer scrutiny.

What he saw was a lot of meaningless doodling, except for one corner. There his manager had penciled in a small tiger next to the letters "M" and "E". He seized the paper with hopeful anticipation while his mind worked over this new possibility. It was only an assumption, he admitted, but . . . what if that animal was symbolic of the Red Tiger, and the initials represented Elizabeth and Martin? What if Damrong had deliberately left a clue?

It left him in the same position as before, for the Chief of Police had already intimated who might have the Thurstons, and Damrong had left no clue of their present whereabouts. He folded the paper, tucked it into his pocket, and then, noticing his torn sleeve, decided to get a clean shirt.

He went up the spiral staircase—his mind still on Damrong's scribblings—entered the lounge, chose a shirt at random from the closet, and then went through a second door that led into his office.

He turned on the desk lamp, dropped his briefcase onto a chair, and then changed shirts—the new one was tan with paler stripes shining in it, reminding him of the tan and red outfit Elizabeth had worn the day they had gone to the floating markets. And she had looked beautiful, he thought with a grin, even with that distrustful gleam in her eyes that intrigued him so. The memory only heightened his determination to find them, and he sat down, opened the briefcase and spread her sketches out on the desk.

He studied them for a long time, trying to get some message, hoping that his eyes would trigger a memory and satisfy the nagging feeling about the Chinese figure. Somewhere, he knew, somewhere he had met that man. But where?

Finally, he sighed in defeat and went to the lounge for a cup of coffee. Bringing it back to his office, he put it down on the desk and began pacing the floor, going over the facts again.

The Thurstons had been kidnapped. Damrong was missing. The police were well-informed. The Red Tiger was involved, as well as a Mr. Wong—who were, perhaps, the same man. That seemed to be the end of a very short list, and Jonas shook his head.

The more he paced, the angrier he became, until he was ready for the first time in his life to tear someone apart. It would give him tremendous satisfaction, he thought, if he could get hold of the man holding the Thurstons and beat him to a puddle of congealed muscle and bone.

"Ah!" he exploded. He was wasting precious time on useless anger, better that he should channel it into positive steps toward a rescue!

But *what* steps, his mind seemed to scream.

He stopped pacing, took a deep breath and mumbled, "Stop it, Adams. You can't think when you panic!"

But, oh how desperately he wanted to find Elizabeth and Martin!

"Lord," he said aloud, shattering the quietness of his office, "I'm not a detective! What kind of a productive search can I make in this crowded, conglomerated city? I don't know what to do!"

Sighing, he reached for his cup and gulped down half the contents, then grimaced. It was definitely left from the previous day, and even hot, tasted old and flat—just the way he felt.

He sat down again and stared at the sketches of his two American friends. From their first meeting, he had been drawn to the calm, gentle pilot, whose unconscious habit of pushing wire-rimmed glasses back on his nose with his thumb amused Jonas. A complete trust and camaraderie had developed so easily between them—an openness that doesn't often happen—and Jonas would gladly claim Martin as the younger brother he'd never had.

And Elizabeth.

Jonas ran an impatient hand over his unruly hair as he thought of her. There was so much he liked, so much he needed in his own life.

"That guy was a fool," he muttered, assessing the young man who had so cruely rejected Elizabeth.

Jonas thought about the death of his young bride. She was far better off now—free of pain and in God's presence—and he had submitted to her absence as an inevitable experience of life. There was no value in bitterness or criticism of God, or even bemoaning his loneliness. He had accepted her death, wept privately, and then gone on with his life of serving God. But the ache, the loneliness, hadn't disappeared; he had merely adjusted.

Elizabeth had then come, though reluctantly, into his life, and in spite of her emotional struggle, he instinctively knew she could fill the void in his heart; she could become part of his very existence. Perhaps, he thought, even more than his quiet, shy Nancy had ever been.

"Let me find them, Lord," he pleaded in a whisper. "Let me get there in time!"

Jonas dropped his head down on his arms spread out on the desk in an attitude of dependency and continued to pray, until finally, he fell into an exhausted, dreamless sleep.

Three hours later, he sat up with the unmistakable knowledge that something had disturbed his sleep. He waited, immobile, listening, searching through the stillness of the empty building for a sound. It was a long, suspended moment, waiting to define the trouble. It could have been the night watchman, but he remembered the regular man had been ill and Damrong was to check for a replacement this week.

Jonas stood up and moved noiselessly to the window overlooking the display room. He couldn't see anyone, but the sensation of another presence was so strong that he felt as though a hand had brushed the back of his neck, and he moved cautiously out the door and down the stairs.

The display room was empty, but he moved guardedly around the wall, checking the smaller offices and listening for intruders. Passing the front window, he noticed that the police jeep was still at the corner, but now it was empty. Were the police in his building for some reason? If so, why hadn't they let him know?

Thinking he heard a slight shuffling in the stock room, he walked quietly in that direction, stood listening at the door; and then, slowly and reluctantly, pushed it open and stepped into the dimmer light.

"Hey! What are you doing?" he almost shouted at the two men in black who were huddled near a large packing crate.

"Who are you?" Jonas demanded, but received no answer. "What do you think you're doing in my building?"

The men just stood looking past his shoulder, ignoring his questions.

Jonas realized they were watching someone behind him, waiting for instructions so he turned for an angry confrontation and at the same time reached for the wall telephone to call the police.

But he was too late!

He had time to see only a dark, indistinguishable shadow behind the door before a thousand sparks were shooting off in his brain, as what felt like the side of the building came crashing down on his head.

He fought the stabbing pain that pounded through his protesting thoughts and staggered to find the door, thinking that he needed those two policemen now. For a few seconds, he fought off the inevitable, but then a blackness began to invade his mind, and slowly, irrevocably, he slumped to the floor.

Damrong turned from the temple doorway to tell Chen that his revolver wasn't needed. "It's just Phil and Viv." then he looked again through the doorway and added, "Sung Yen is with them." He leaned against the wall, waiting for the trio to enter the room, but not bothering to greet them as they filed in.

Elizabeth dropped her head on Martin's shoulder; she wasn't particularly thrilled to see Viv. She was tired from a restless night, her head still ached with fever, and the uncertainties of the near future still played upon her mind. She knew she wanted to give a positive affirmation of her faith in the hours that were left, but didn't know how she could face more sarcasm, and winced at the girl's grating voice.

"Good morning, superman," Viv said, walking toward Martin, ignoring Elizabeth in another attempt to arouse some response from him. Adopting a sultry voice, she put a consoling hand on his shoulder. "You don't look as though you got much sleep last night. Weren't the accommodations satisfactory?"

"No worse than one might expect," Martin replied evenly, disregarding her closeness to watch the two men who had come with her.

Phil didn't speak, but threw a sympathetic look toward Elizabeth and, with the help of Sung Yen, began setting up breakfast for the two prisoners. He carried an "eastern lunch pail"—a set of four porcelain dishes, nesting one in the other, and topped by a lid and handle. Martin remembered many of those from his childhood and knew it meant a hot meal. That, along with the tea in the thermos Sung Yen brought in, would help them get rid of the night's chill and revive them a little.

Damrong untied Elizabeth's hands and her soft "Thanks" triggered a mocking response from Viv, who, being rebuffed by Martin, had crossed the room to sit down.

"How polite!" she laughed, then anger filled her face. "Don't you have any backbone? After spending the night in this wet, God-forsaken plàce, haven't you enough guts to even get angry!"

Elizabeth smiled slightly, her expression calm and confident, even though the girl's attitude rubbed at her tired spirits. "But, don't you know," she said patiently, as though explaining something to a child, "God hasn't forsaken us."

Viv groaned and mumbled some derogatory remark while she watched Martin flex the night's stiffness from his hands. "Did you try to get loose?" she asked with interest, looking pointedly at the red, raw stripes around his wrists.

"Wouldn't you?" he responded evenly.

"You bet I would!" She turned then to Damrong. "You and Chen are wanted by the boss in town."

"Now?" Damrong asked, a little surprised. He looked as though he didn't trust the girl, and turned to her companion for confirmation.

Phil nodded. "The last thing Wong said was that you were to get back to the city as soon as we got here."

"Why?"

Phil shrugged. "Who knows?" he answered dispiritedly, and handed Elizabeth a plate of Indian bread, sprinkled liberally with sugar and rolled up like a Mexican burrito. "You're to wait for him at the warehouse, and he said you had better be there."

"Where is he now?"

Again Phil shrugged. "I don't know."

Damrong seemed reluctant to leave, and after a long hesitation, glanced toward the door leading to the next room where the water had risen level with the threshold. Martin watched his face, looking for something that would reveal his thoughts, but it was a study of indifference and left Martin unprepared for what happened next.

Damrong hadn't moved, but he said commandingly, "Chen, your gun!"

Martin followed Damrong's gaze and stiffened as he watched a long, black snake crawl slowly from the water into the room where they sat.

Chen didn't like to kill animals of any kind, but had no reservations about disposing of the poisonous viper—its head lifted in apparent pursuit, heading straight toward him.

He whispered what probably was a Chinese oath, whipped out his gun and took careful aim. Everyone else waited, immobilized with shock, not daring to move for fear of drawing the snake's attention but silently pleading with Chen to squeeze the trigger before it was too late.

When the gun went off, the noise seemed to bounce off every wall and Elizabeth jerked back in pain, unable to cover her ears for she was mesmerized by the life-threatening creature now slithering toward Damrong.

The snake was hit, but it began to coil its body up for a strike. Chen fired once more, and it lurched out, attempting to reach Damrong for retribution. It writhed and thrashed about, heading first toward Viv and then toward Martin, still trying to make a strike.

One more feeble coiling effort and it lay stretched out, longer than a man's arm, on the floor at Damrong's feet.

"Is it dead?" Viv whispered, her mask of toughness gone, her face white with fear.

Damrong took several steps back from the snake as Chen reached for a piece of rock near his feet and threw it at the still form. It didn't move.

"It's dead," Damrong said and motioned for Chen to get rid of it immediately.

Elizabeth shuddered and turned away; she couldn't watch as Chen kicked the snake back into the water in the next room. Was it true that when you found one snake, you often found its mate? She felt as though something was crawling over her skin and looked down at her food with stomach-churning distaste, quickly setting it aside.

Everyone but Damrong seemed visibly affected by the

presence of the lethal creature. Elizabeth heard Chen speak sharply to Sung Yen and saw him make a hasty exit through the outer door, leaving no doubt about his readiness to return to the city. Sung Yen reached into his jacket, pulled out his gun and retreated to the safest corner of the room where he could watch for other snakes in the advancing flood waters. Phil sat down suddenly beside Viv and put a shaking hand to his face, then turned to see that she had recovered enough from her fear to make some scoffing remarks about the courageous Christians in the group.

Elizabeth was grateful for Martin's supportive arm and sank back against the wall to regain her composure. She closed her eyes as Martin began an instinctive prayer of thanksgiving.

"Father," he said in a firm voice, "thank you for Your protection and for guarding our lives."

When he looked up, Damrong was standing at the doorway preparing to leave, his glance sweeping over everyone in the room. As he turned to leave Martin called, "Damrong, God go with you."

The young man hesitated, perhaps battling the urge to turn toward these friends of Jonas Adams. But without a word or even a backward glance, he left the temple, and shortly afterward they heard the motorboat move off toward the city.

Elizabeth felt as though a bit of their precarious safety had gone with him, and yet she couldn't reconcile his apparent alliance with Wong.

"Liz," Martin said, interrupting her thoughts, "you've got to eat something more." He handed her a plate of fried rice. "The Lord only knows what this day will bring, and we need all the strength we can get."

"I'm not your *Lord,*" Viv spoke up rudely, "but I know what's going to happen to you." Leaning forward she spoke her next words with such sharp clarity that they seemed to echo around the room. "You're going to die today!"

Phil shook his head. "Viv, don't you ever know when to keep your mouth shut?"

"If you don't shut yours, I'll tell Sung Yen to throw you in there with the rest of the snakes!" She jerked a thumb toward the flooded room.

Phil's laugh was short. "I doubt that you could get him that close to the water. He's sitting there waiting for the next snake to appear."

"Well," Viv said harshly, "I hope he's a good shot!"

Martin put his plate down on the ledge and reached for a cup of tea. "What makes you say we're going to die today?" It wasn't a pleasant subject, he thought, but it was far better to be prepared.

Viv drew herself up with a look of self-importance. "Wong said he was going to leave you two tied up in here. You'll either drown in the flood waters or be bitten by a snake like the one we just saw."

Elizabeth shuddered but said nothing, and she heard Martin sigh patiently. "Viv," he said, "you ought to know by now that nothing happens to God's children without His permission. We're not going to die here if He wants us to live; but if we die, then we'll be in His presence forever!"

"How can there be a God with that kind of power!" Viv's voice shook with anger. "If there is a God, and if He has power, then why am I in the mess I'm in? Why doesn't He help me?" Behind the derisive tone Elizabeth thought she detected a plea to prove what they believed.

"I went to church every Sunday of the year when I was a little girl, and never once . . . never once," Viv shouted, "did God ever bother to answer my prayers!"

"Perhaps, that's because you didn't know His Son."

"You mean Jesus? Of course, I know Him. He was born

in Bethlehem, became a religious teacher when He was thirty, and was killed on a cross when He was thirty-three.''

"That's not what I mean," Martin said. "The Bible tells us so much more about Jesus.''

"Give me one good reason why I should believe the Bible," Viv challenged, leaning forward again with an intentness that was unusual.

"One good reason?"

"Yes!"

"Jesus Christ."

"Jesus Christ what?" she spat at him.

"Jesus Christ *is* the reason," he replied patiently. "There are about 50 or 60 major prophecies in the Bible about Him, and there has never been a man—ever—who fulfilled all of them. There's as much chance of that happening as there is for you to reach into a barrel of money and pull out a specially marked nickel.''

"So what?" Viv didn't believe his argument, but she wasn't ready to dismiss the subject.

"So, if He is the only one who fulfilled them all, then we have to believe what He said to us.''

"And," Elizabeth interjected, "He said, 'I am the way, the truth and the life, no man comes to the Father but by me.' If you want eternal life, Viv you must accept Jesus Christ as your Savior.''

Clearly, she felt pushed into a corner, and so she struck out at Elizabeth. "Well, listen to who's talking, the girl who turned bitter because her boyfriend threw her out. Can't take a little rejection, eh?" She waited for that same crushed expression she had seen on Elizabeth's face the day before and was puzzled when it didn't appear. She just couldn't let go of the subject; it replaced the uncomfortable discussion she was having with Martin about God.

"Yesterday," she said accusingly, "you were very bitter, and you can't deny it. That's not being Christian, is it?"

"Yes, I was bitter," Elizabeth said, setting her plate of half-eaten food down. "But I'm not any more."

"Why not? Are you getting rid of your sins before you die? Are you preparing to meet your God?"

Phil turned in swift reaction, reached out and shook Viv hard by the shoulders. "What's the matter with you? Do you have to dig and dig at people? Viv, for heaven's sake, keep still!"

His burst of anger surprised Viv more than anyone else, and her eyes widened as she listened, but when he saw the cunning look spreading over her face and her mouth open to make another comment, he spoke again. "Just keep quiet. I've heard enough of your sarcasm. If you can't believe in God, stop needling those who do! Besides, Viv, you don't have any guarantee you're going to make it through this day either."

"I do! Wong promised! He said he was sending us out of the country on their passports! You heard what he said." Viv's voice rose in fear as she tried to convince herself that they would soon be out of Wong's grasp. "He said he would do it today. We're supposed to wear their clothes and change our hair styles to look more like their passport pictures. He said so, he promised!"

Phil sank back against the wall and looked down at the floor. "After all the tricks you've seen that man pull, after all the killings he's ordered, you really don't trust his word, do you? You know very well that he lives to manipulate people and situations. Crushing someone else's spirit by broken promises gives him a perverted kind of happiness."

But Viv wasn't to be diverted from her faith in an imminent escape nor in her desire to punish Elizabeth as much as possible.

"Well, Little Miss Innocence, does it make you feel better to have such an admirer? It's too bad you're not going to live long enough to enjoy all this worship." She moved away from Phil, curling up in a corner to keep out of his reach. "Tell me why you've had a change of heart."

Elizabeth studied the girl for a moment, wanting so much to share with her the peace she felt. "I think," she began slowly, "that you understand how bitter I felt, because you really feel rejected by God, and its about to tear you apart inside."

Viv's head jerked up as though someone had struck her, but Elizabeth didn't wait for a verbal response. "Last night, or rather, early this morning, I faced the fact that my bitterness was putting a wall between God and me. I was tired of letting it fill my thoughts and rule my emotions. I wanted peace."

Viv was intrigued; this was a new concept. "So?"

"I gave to God all my rights, especially the right not to be hurt or rejected by someone I loved. I belong to God, and whatever He brings into my life is all right." Elizabeth leaned forward sympathetically. "Don't you understand, Viv, that you can only be truly happy when you have a right relationship with the One who made you?"

"That sounds like someone who is giving in."

"You're right, it is. But I'm giving in to One who is more powerful than I. He can control situations; He can take us from this temple alive, if He wants. If I truly believe that, even though I may not enjoy what's happening, then I can be at peace."

Viv shook her head in disbelief. "You're a nut, do you know that? A nut!"

Sung Yen, who had been silently following the conversation, perhaps unable to follow all of the English but understanding a little, sat up straight and motioned for them to be quiet.

"Boat comes," he said, moving cautiously toward the doorway. His next words sent a chill through Elizabeth and she reached for Martin's hand. "Wong here now."

The moment Wong entered the room, sharply dressed in a dark blue suit and looking as immaculate as ever, the atmosphere was charged with tension. Viv shrank back into her corner, the hostile expression on her face indicating she was prepared to fight every inch of her way to freedom. Phil looked even more dispirited and sad than he had previously, but he sat watching Wong with a wary eye.

Elizabeth felt apprehension spread through her with the same speed that the swollen, turbulent river was rushing past the temple, and she prayed silently for continued peace of mind and heart. Even Martin sat a little straighter as he saw the man approaching.

Wong smiled and greeted everyone pleasantly, enjoying the entrance he had made. Moving slowly around the room, he increased the tension he had created. First, he stopped to stare silently at Viv, laughed silently at the fire sparkling in her eyes, then moved on to intimidate Phil with the same routine, finally walking deliberately over to the ledge where Elizabeth and Martin sat.

"Did you spend a pleasant night?" he asked, reaching out to tip Elizabeth's chin up so that he might look her full-in-the-face, knowing how much she hated his touch.

She saw Martin's free hand curl up into a right fist and squeezed the hand she held in warning. Suffering Wong's scrutiny was a little matter at the moment, and she didn't want Martin getting hurt needlessly.

"Did you send us out here for a pleasant night?" she asked boldly.

"No," he said, amused at her temerity. "I sent you out here because I had been warned the police were going to raid my home and my warehouse."

"And did they?"

"Yes, this morning after Phil and Viv left."

"How clever of you," Elizabeth said, turning her head

to get rid of that hand still touching her face.

"Not really," he said, his eyes still lingering over her face from her blue eyes, her pale cheeks, down to her lips. "Too bad," he said softly. "You are quite pretty." He stood over her, a finger moving down her cheek, and his eyes shifted to Martin, whose face had turned white with anger. "You had better not move a muscle in your sister's defense, my friend. The guard I brought with me this morning is young, reckless, and trigger-happy."

The guard stood just inside the doorway, a gun in his hand, ready to use it the moment he was instructed. He was the most cruel-looking of all of Wong's guards, and Elizabeth didn't doubt for a moment that he would shoot to kill at even a flick of Wong's hand.

No one moved. Wong was the principal actor on the stage and all thoughts were wholly taken up with what he would do or say next.

He waited until he finally saw a pleading look come slowly into Elizabeth's eyes. He nodded in amused satisfaction that he had made her beg for her brother's safety and turned away.

"Now then, we must finish our preparations for today. I have sent Damrong and Chen on a little errand, and in just a few moments, we'll be leaving . . ." His words were cut off by the sound of rocks falling into the river as part of the old building shifted from the force of the river current.

"The temple is falling apart!" Viv shouted and jumped to her feet, ready to run for safety, even going to Phil for protection.

But Wong was at the door giving instructions to Sung Yen. He turned and looked at the four Americans who were his prisoners and spoke to the young Chinese beside him.

"Tie those two up," he said, pointing to one couple,

"and put the other two in the boat."

In the stunned silence that followed his orders, Elizabeth went weak with the disbelief and revulsion that swept over her. How could he do it? How could he stand there and so coldly order the inevitable death of two human beings? She looked at Martin, her eyes wide with grief. "Lord, help us," she whispered.

An insistent, jarring summons jabbed into Jonas' mind like streaks of lightning, and he groaned in protest. Why was he hearing an alarm clock, when he didn't even own one? With his eyes closed against the ache in his head, he groped around, ineffectively searching for the offensive instrument.

Suddenly, he realized it wasn't an alarm, but a telephone, and he wasn't in his bed, but lying—cold and uncomfortable—on the floor, his head propped against something hard. He cautiously opened his eyes just a fraction, testing their ability to function, and what he saw brought the cause of his present misery flooding back into his mind.

He struggled to stand, groaning at the reeling pain that made it difficult for him to reach for the telephone. Leaning heavily against the counter and exploring the tender spot on his head, he picked up the receiver.

"Adams Exports," he mumbled, still feeling his way past his distress into full consciousness.

"You'll find them at the old Nakornmai Temple on the river."

Jonas stood straight up in surprise, then sucked in his breath at the throbbing pain aggravated by the sudden movement.

"Damrong! Thank the Lord! Where are you? What's happened?"

Jonas' immediate reaction to his friend's voice was one of tremendous relief. Now he would have help; now he would rescue the Thurstons.

"Damrong?" he repeated against the silence on the other end of the line.

"The old Nakornmai Temple," his assistant whispered.

Then Jonas heard a click and the line went dead.

"Damrong! Wait, don't hang up! Damrong!"

For a long moment, Jonas could not comprehend the swift reversal of events that took him so abruptly from elation to despair. The change, coming so unexpectedly, left him bemused, and it was several minutes before Damrong's information made the impact that was intended.

Jonas hung up the receiver, and in spite of unsteady movements, pushed away from the counter and examined the large crate where the intruders had been standing. It didn't appear to have been touched and he wondered what they had been doing. It was then that Damrong's words exploded in his mind.

"The temple!" he said aloud. It was five in the morning by the wall clock, and he regretted he couldn't make the trip in darkness. He would just have to take his chances in approaching the temple unseen.

Bursting out of the stock room, he started to get his car keys from his office but had to stop part way up the stairs to let the pain in his head subside. A couple of aspirins would have to take care of that, he thought, for he didn't intend taking precious time to be checked at the clinic.

In his office, he picked up his keys and then remembered the gun he kept in the safe. He had been an avid hunter as a youth, but he had never even taken aim at a human being. He hoped he wouldn't have to do so now.

Back downstairs at the front door, he hesitated, wondering what he would do about his police escort. Without question, he was adamant about one thing—no one was going to prevent him getting to the Thurstons. Traffic on the river would be fairly active soon, and with God's grace, he might get near the temple without being seen. If he could avoid the police, he just might get to the Thurstons.

"Lord, give me wisdom," he prayed. "I don't want to walk into a trap or do anything foolish, but I have to go."

Having settled his intentions in his mind, he stepped out on the sidewalk, locked the door and went to his car, hardly glancing at the police jeep, hoping the men weren't there.

When he pulled out into the street, he glanced into the rear view mirror to see two men in brown khaki uniforms racing down the street toward their jeep. Just maybe, he would be fortunate enough to get to the river before they caught up with him, he thought.

In his intense concentration on getting away from the police and to the temple, he hadn't given much thought to the activities of those who had broken into his stock room. That didn't seem too important at the moment, but he decided that as soon as he got the Thurstons he would check in with Prince Chandruang.

He kept the accelerator to the floor as much as possible, gathering speed whenever he could and taking the corners like a race car driver. When he got to the nearest pier along the river, he jumped out of the car, locked it hurriedly and sprinted down to the water's edge to search for a boat he might rent. He wanted one that was fast and partially covered to conceal his presence.

One sweeping glance told him that he wasn't going to find a particularly fast one, but there were several filled with merchandise. If he rented one of those, he might not look too conspicious when he arrived at the temple.

He heard tires squealing in the distance as he approached the owner of a boat, pulled a wad of Thai money from his pocket, and called out in Thai that he would buy the man's boat and bring it back to the pier if he could.

He didn't wait for any protests, but thrust the large amount of money into the startled man's hands and jumped down into the boat. With one swift motion he pulled the starter cord on the motor and pushed away from the pier.

He glanced over his shoulder and saw the boat owner was quite happily counting his money but, as yet, there was no sign of the police.

Jonas turned back to concentrate on the job of maneuvering around several other smaller boats heading toward the morning floating markets. The river current was strong and he had to be careful that he didn't get in anyone's way.

When traffic had thinned out slightly, he checked over his shoulder. No sign of the police yet.

The boat swept slowly past the familiar tourist sights now gleaming in the early morning sun, the bridge to Thonburi, and finally the outskirts of the city.

Just visible at a wide section in the river sat the crumbling Buddhist temple, looking desolate and forboding. The land immediately surrounding the building was flooded; there was no other access than on that long, wooden pier where he would be totally exposed and vulnerable to attack. Getting up to the temple unseen seemed an impossible task; one idle glance out of the entranceway by a guard and it would be the end.

"I've got to get in there undetected!" he said aloud. "But how?"

Perhaps, he thought, noticing a boat just ahead laden down with sheets of raw rubber and moving leisurely but noisily upstream, perhaps it would shield him for awhile.

He pulled his boat in close behind the other and smiled a friendly greeting at the startled teenager guiding the rubber-filled boat. The boy took a quick look at him, swallowed hard, and turned away, deciding it wiser to ignore a tag-along boat piloted by a foreigner.

Jonas reached down to rummage through some clothes he had noticed on the floor and picked up a woven hat. It seemed inadequate, but perhaps it would do. He wrinkled his nose at the choice odors emanating from the clothes and hat, but if it helped his cause, he didn't care.

"Now for the hard part," he muttered, as he slowed down to allow the other boat to move on ahead.

"God protect me," he prayed, feeling extremely vulnerable as he cut the motor back to allow the boat to drift ashore. Somehow, if he was not to be discovered momentarily, he needed a diversion.

And without warning, it came.

The sky seemed to split open to pour a drenching rain down on the world about him, just as though the Lord had reached out to hang a sheet of water about his boat. He could barely see the temple and was surprised when the boat bumped hard against the pier, nearly knocking him off-balance.

With his heart pounding in anticipation of a confrontation, he threw a rope over a post and jumped out of the boat.

Running, dodging rotting wood, crouching low, he waited for a burst of gunfire that would cut him down like harvested rice. He expected it—in spite of the downpour, in spite of his trust in God's protection. The swollen river was level with the pier and made his progress extremely treacherous.

He paused at the open doorway to catch his breath and pull the gun from his pocket. What waited for him just around the corner of that entranceway, he didn't know, but he expected at least two guards. He hoped that his two friends were out of the line of fire for, like it or not, he would use his weapon if necessary.

Discarding the Thai hat, he shot a quick, silent prayer heavenward, took a deep breath, and burst through the inner door, crouching low for protection, gun aimed and ready for action against his prospective enemies.

What he saw stopped him dead in his tracks. "What are you two doing here?"

The two people tied to a metal pole along one ledge stared at him in surprise.

"Where's Elizabeth and Martin?" he shouted, waving his gun at the two, pressuring them for a response.

Finally, Phil spoke. "Wong has them."

"But I was told they were here."

"They *were,*" the girl said bitterly, "but Wong changed his mind."

"What do you mean?" Jonas asked, taking a step further into the room.

"He told me he was going to leave them here," Viv said, a string of oaths spilling from her mouth. "That dirty liar, he promised that we could leave the country on their passports today!"

"But where did he take the Thurstons?" Jonas asked impatiently.

"Are you going to shoot me if I don't tell?" Viv asked.

Jonas looked down at the gun in his hand, then tucked it under his belt. "Of course not. But where are they? I must find them!"

"Well, well, you must be another knight in shining armor, come to rescue the fair maiden. Are you one of those Christians, too?"

"Look, those two people mean a lot to me. Please tell me where they are."

"Will you get on your knees?" she asked spitefully, then laughed almost hysterically. "I wouldn't tell you if you were the King of Thailand!"

Phil opened his mouth to give Jonas the information he

wanted, but Viv interrupted with a screaming reaction, lifting her foot and bringing it down with a hard *thud* on Phil's foot.

"You keep your mouth shut! I don't care if he never finds them. Why should they get all the breaks, when we're going to die in this . . . this hole! Phil, if you tell him anything, even one word, I'll get loose from here and strangle you, I swear it!"

On and on she ranted, first at Phil and Wong, blaming them for all the misery she had recently endured, and finally directing her animosity toward God. Leaning forward in despair she screamed at the ceiling.

"God, do you hear me? You have no right to do this to me! What have I ever done to you? Why are you so cruel; why haven't you ever spoken to me or helped me? Listen to me, God!"

Realizing she was going beyond reason in her anger, Jonas crossed to her quickly to grip her by the shoulders. "Stop it!" he ordered, giving her a hard shake. "Stop it now!"

Her words broke off in mid-sentence and she stared up at him silently for a moment, then burst into tears.

Jonas spoke to Phil, who sat miserably and helplessly tied to the metal rod watching Viv fall apart emotionally. "I'll get you out of here," he promised, "but you must tell me where to find the Thurstons."

"Never," Viv screamed, now almost delirious. "Never, never, never!"

"Then, I'll leave you here to die," he replied decisively and turned to leave, hoping that Phil would break away from Viv's domination and tell him what he wanted to know.

Just as he got to the door, the building trembled slightly and shifted on its foundation, water from the other room rushing in toward them. The force of the river current was going to tear the temple apart.

"You haven't much time," he said, turning once more. "Do you want out of here?"

Viv's eyes were wide with fear; her anger had dissolved rapidly in the face of death. "Do something, Phil," she whimpered and leaned against him weakly. "Do something, quick!"

Phil glanced down at their restraints and then up at Jonas. "Please, help us. I don't think we have much time!"

Jonas was across the room before Phil finished speaking, beginning to untie the ropes. "Where are they?"

"Wong is going to take them to the airport this morning. I'm not sure of the time, but they're going to accompany some shipment you're sending out."

The danger of being trapped in the temple pressed at Jonas but the ropes were wet and hampered his work. "That would be at 9 o'clock. I've got a large order flying out to America. Do you know where they've gone now?"

"No. Somewhere so they can get cleaned up and change clothes. I doubt that it would be at the warehouse; Wong knows the police are there."

"Why is he sending the Thurstons with that shipment?"

Phil was free of his ropes and tried to help Jonas work on the ones still binding Viv to the rod. "It's full of opium," he muttered.

"Dear Lord," Jonas whispered. "The police could shoot them without even bothering to ask questions unless I'm there!"

"Is there something we can do for you, Mr. Adams?" a voice asked from the entranceway.

Jonas turned his head sharply and saw his two police friends standing just inside the door.

"Yes, you can take these two down to police headquarters."

The two men moved into the room to take charge and

Jonas stepped back to let them work on Viv's ropes. He moved back toward the door, his mind working quickly. If he stopped to tell the entire story, they would see that he didn't get near the airport; he had to leave without them. Hoping no one would notice, he edged closer to the door.

Viv was screaming for them to hurry, for the room was filling rapidly with the flood waters.

At that moment, she was free of her ropes and erupted off the ledge like a wild cat, screaming and clawing and trying to get away from the police. It was just the opportunity Jonas needed, for it took all three men to contain her.

Silently, he slipped out of the temple, determined to get to his boat before he was missed. It was a treacherous walk down the pier; some of it was washed away, and all of it was under water. He crawled, sloshed, and scrambled, going from post to post, sheer determination preventing him from being washed away by the overwhelming current.

He felt part of the pier give way, made a wild grab for the rope, pulled hard and literally fell into his boat. Not stopping to look back or even to check himself for injuries, he crawled to the motor and gave a quick tug on the cord. When it failed to catch, he groaned and pulled again—hard.

This time it caught, and he sighed in relief as he guided the boat around and headed back toward Bangkok. Out in the middle of the river, he looked over his shoulder and was relieved to see that the others had made it out of the temple and were running the flooded gauntlet to get to their boat. After that, he dismissed the group from his mind and concentrated on getting back to the right pier without mishap. He didn't want to end up in the river, nor did he care to smash into other river vessels. He was going with the current now, and it made for a speedier, but more dangerous trip.

Anxiously he watched the shore, looking for familiar

landmarks. He thought he could recognize the right place, but was greatly relieved when he saw his car, and pulled in near the pier, cut the motor, and threw the rope to the same man with whom he had made his hurried transaction.

Leaping from the boat, he cupped his hands together and raised them chest-high, thanked the boat owner in Thai, and dashed up the pier to his car, leaving the man more assured than ever that foreigners were crazy.

Figuring that the police were less than ten minutes behind him and that it would take them at least that long to get Phil and Viv down to headquarters, he thought he had not more than a fifteen-minute head start. He took less than ten at his office to change clothes.

He ignored the need to shave, grabbed the first outfit he could find in the closet—a pair of navy blue trousers and a white, Thai shirt—pulled his wet shoes off for a pair of well-worn loafers, and started out of the lounge when he remembered the gun still with his wet clothes which lay in a puddle on the closet floor. He took time to lock it in his safe, knowing it would jeopardize other lives at the airport and be a detriment in any rescue attempt.

Glancing at his watch, he saw that he had about one hour to get through the heavy airport traffic before that shipment was loaded on a plane—unless the crates were still in the stock room.

He took the steps two at a time, and pushed open the stock room door, half expecting to see the crates where they had been left for the weekend. They were gone.

That meant that Damrong had been by to pick them up. The thought brought Jonas up short as he stood staring at the empty place on the floor. Wong's men could have gotten back into the building to take the crates, but he was suddenly wondering if it had been his assistant? If so, did that mean Damrong was working for Wong? He wouldn't get the answers standing there alone, so he walked quickly through the display room, checked through the front windows for the presence of the police, and then slid cautiously through the front door and out to his car.

He had a feeling he was rushing headlong down a mountainside and that what awaited him at the airport would end this nightmare, one way or the other.

He was sure it would be like the experience most people wonder about when they search the hidden places of their own souls; when they alternately dread the confrontation or fantasize their victories. That time when man knowingly puts his personal courage to the test, wondering if it will withstand the pressure, fearing it might break and reveal weakness, knowing that in the end, courage will stand stripped and defeated unless the soul is upheld by the hand of God himself.

"Even though I walk through . . . I will fear no evil," he thought as he pulled the car out into the street and headed toward the airport.

"I will fear no evil."

Nine

The drive to the airport was as frustratingly slow as he had feared, and what Jonas saw when he finally dashed into the vast concrete building marked "Air Freight Terminal" was far from encouraging—it was chaotic.

It looked as though there was a representative of every business in Bangkok waiting to see their goods through two cramped customs gates where the officials were setting their own maddening, measured pace. In addition, there was an unusual number of laborers—some with heavy loads exiting through the wide doorways leading to waiting aircraft and returning empty-handed. Jonas had been in the terminal hundreds of times and didn't remember ever seeing it so crowded or hectic. There were too many people around, too many lives that would be endangered should problems arise. And he had an unshakable feeling there would be trouble.

He paused just inside the door to get his bearings and glance quickly over the room in hopes of spotting the Thurstons, his anger at being a pawn in a situation he didn't understand surging to the surface. He wasn't in any condition, he argued silently with the Lord, for a complicated altercation; his mind was utterly exhausted from lack of sleep, being knocked unconscious, and the continuous tension of momentarily expecting to be shot. He tried to whip up his sagging strength, knowing he would need every ounce of energy he might have in reserve. When God put him out on a limb, would He really fulfill His promise that His strength would be perfected in man's weakness? Jonas prayed that it would be so.

But it was disadvantageous to stand waiting to be discovered, so he stepped forward to begin his search down one side of the room. Just as quickly he halted as someone shoved him against the wall to avoid disasterous contact with a massive wooden crate that bore down on him from the left. At first glance, its only connection to the floor was a pair of skinny legs in tattered tennis shoes, but the rest of the laborer's frail body emerged from underneath as he carried the crate away. Jonas shook his head, always amazed at how much weight those slender bodies could handle.

Turning back to the problem of finding the Thurstons, he encountered long lines of customers—Chinese men in the typical business attire of dark trousers and white shirts waving identification papers at placid officials, turbaned *Sikhs* with full, bushy beards calling loudly for attention, Thai delivery men calmly waiting their turn—all of them sandwiched in between separate stacks of cardboard boxes, slatted crates and metal drums. It was difficult to separate the mixture of man and merchandise in order to find his two friends, and it didn't help that he had to continually dodge the flow of traffic and stop to apologize for colliding into people. He jostled with men intent on bettering their positions, barely missed being sideswiped by a figure careening down the aisle in a determined effort to deliver a mound of carelessly stacked cartons, and avoided several security men standing guard.

He was beginning to think he had been given false information by Viv and Phil and was even contemplating some form of mild punishment for them when, on his way back down the confused lines of customers, he finally spotted Elizabeth.

The relief of finding her—after the wildest night he had ever spent—brought him to a sudden stop, and he took a moment to savor his gratitude, greedily taking in the sight of her, acknowledging that she had become incredibly important in his life. This woman, that he had known for such a short time, this one who fought his friendship like a terrified kitten—had come like a small explosion into his life and he knew he would never be the same.

He digested all this in the seconds before his eyes shifted reluctantly to study the surrounding scene. His shipment of four sizeable crates was stacked at the end of the line, just in front of the exit doors leading out to the apron where a parked C-130 was being loaded. Elizabeth stood, one hand on an open crate, her profile revealing an utter weariness and misery. Even from where he stood, he could see that she was nervous and tense, jerking each time a customs official waved a lacquered bowl at Martin who stood on the opposite side of the crates from his sister. Jonas' eyebrows shot up in surprise as Martin spoke vigorously to the officer—he had never seen his new pilot so articulate. He couldn't hear what was being said, but it was obvious by Martin's actions that he was defending Jonas. It was a sobering scene, and even more disturbing were the three grim-faced security guards standing on the far side of the crates facing Jonas, intently watching Martin. Hands on their hips, they looked as though they were within an inch of using their guns.

Just then, as if feeling his gaze, Elizabeth turned her

head and looked straight into his eyes, but instead of registering relief as he had expected, she was dismayed, and frowningly shook her head, a hand at her side warning him away.

Undaunted by the signal, Jonas began working his way down the line, squirming in between boxes and trying to ignore the silent, disapproving looks he received because of his unkempt appearance. He bowed slightly to an older, baldheaded Chinese who was irritated at the interruption until he recognized Jonas. A fellow-exporter who was obviously curious about his strange behavior tried to strike up a lengthy conversation. Jonas hurriedly excused himself, promising to meet soon for lunch—if he were still alive by then, he thought silently. His glance returned again and again to Elizabeth who had edged carefully away from the argument by the crates and now hurried to meet him.

"Jonas, please get out of here! It's a trap!" She pushed inadequately at his arm, determined that he not get any closer. "Go, before they see you!" Her lips quivered, her blue eyes filled with tears as she looked up into his face, and she wished for the luxury of being held in his arms while she released the flood of tears she had been holding back all night. Wong was about to have his way, she thought desperately, and there was nothing she could do about it!

"Liz," Jonas said, a soft smile sweeping away the fatigue in his eyes and the exhaustion pulling at his mouth. "I've spent all night looking for you; you can't get rid of me that easily."

Now that God had answered his request to locate the Thurstons, he felt the calmness and confidence for which he had been praying. For a moment the rest didn't seem to matter. Then another thought crossed his mind and he frowned down at her upturned face, searching it for evidence of what she had endured.

"Are you all right? Did anyone hurt you?"

"I'm fine," she replied, surprised at the forbidding expression on his face that said he wouldn't take it lightly if someone had harmed her.

A quiver in her voice caused him to question her reply, but he let it go for the moment. He was so relieved to see her that he ignored any protests she might make, and putting an arm around her waist, drew her closer, kissed her lightly on the forehead, then looked down into her face, his eyes searching for her response.

What he saw increased his smile. "The wall is down," he said softly, seeing no bitterness or resentment in her expression.

Elizabeth's forehead creased in a slight frown, her eyes widened in confusion for a second and then, understanding that he was referring to her attempt to keep others at a distance, said, "Yes . . . I . . . It's OK . . . Jonas . . . I . . ." lowering her eyes in confusion as she tried to tell him what she had decided.

"We'll talk about it later," he interrupted, smiling again, and the look that passed between them made Elizabeth catch her breath in wonder.

She came back down to earth when he turned to move forward. With fear in her eyes, she gripped his arm and held back. "Jonas, don't you understand? There's opium in your shipment. It's loaded with it. They're going to arrest you!" He felt her trembling slightly. "Wong is going to start a riot, hoping that he'll get people so angry, they'll demand you be shot right here! Please, leave before they see you!"

"So that's what went on in my stock room last night!" It suddenly made a lot of sense, and Jonas was appalled that he hadn't thought of such an entrapment before this. From the rumors circulating in the city ever since he had arrived, he should have been forewarned. He had heard about opium being found in the merchandise of an European exporter who, though never proven guilty beyond doubt, had sold out and moved out of the country. Other stories about the Red Tiger were rampant, how he killed without mercy, how he seemed to make the Caucasian businessmen his target, how he had enough power to paralyze his countrymen into submission. If Wong was not the man they called the Red Tiger, he certainly was a good student of his tactics.

Jonas knew that his only excuse for not being more prudent was his intense concern for the Thurstons. If he had to make a decision between his business and a fellow human being, he knew what the choice would be. However, he also realized that much more was at stake than Adams Exports. Every friend, every Christian organization stood to lose face if he were found guilty of this crime. Too many people counted on him; too much of God's work would suffer.

"Jonas, please go!" Elizabeth begged earnestly, her hands on his chest trying to push him away.

He took her hands in his and held them so tightly she winced. His face was a study of intense determination. "Elizabeth," he said slowly, looking down into her face again, "I can't leave."

That was the first time he hadn't used her nickname; Elizabeth looked at him in surprise. He must feel more concern over this matter than she had hoped, and that frightened her. She had been unconsciously counting on him coming to save them and making everything right. Had she been expecting too much? A chill swept over her, and her stomach knotted painfully, bringing on an uncontrollable trembling.

"Wong kidnapped you Sunday night?"

"Yes, we were at his warehouse and then in a temple on the river . . ."

Jonas nodded. "The Nakornmai."

"How did you know?"

"Damrong called me early this morning and I went out there after you."

"Oh! What happened?"

"The place almost caved in before I got out. Phil and Viv were determined not to tell me that Wong was bringing you here. Where is he, by the way?"

"In this room somewhere, and he's threatened to kill us if we try to get away."

Jonas steeled himself not to take a quick look around the room until he heard Elizabeth's soft gasp. "Jonas, look!"

He glanced up and saw she was referring to the fact that as they moved closer to Martin, they had become a small island in a room full of silent, wary people who tried to get as far away as possible without missing the drama, while three more security men circled around behind them.

As they stepped up to the crates, Jonas put a hand on Elizabeth's arm and guided her nearer Martin. If he was to be a target of Wong's gun, he didn't want her in the way. Then he followed Thai custom and raised his folded hands chest high as he greeted the men waiting for him.

"Good morning. I'm Jonas Adams. Is there some difficulty with my merchandise?"

"Mr. Adams," the customs officer spoke sharply, "you are shipping this to the United States?"

"Yes, that's correct."

"We have found opium in it, and you are under arrest. Please wait here until the police arrive."

"Would it be possible for us to move to a private office?" Jonas inquired politely, hoping to get away from the crowds. "This is hampering your work." He glanced significantly around the room where every activity had stopped as customer and worker alike watched the scene with open curiosity and avid interest.

"Jonas." Martin spoke for the first time to his employer. "We can't move from here."

"Why not?"

"Wong has Damrong and if we leave this spot before the police arrive, he's threatened to kill him." Martin's words, though quietly spoken, carried across the silent audience and several men grunted in surprise, edging even further away from possible danger.

Jonas' mouth went dry as he realized one more person might die because of him, and an acute anger sharpened his weary mind into intense concentration. He was going to make every effort to see that that didn't happen.

"What is this?" the Thai official demanded, raising a hand to signal the guards into action. "What are you talking about? Who is here with a gun?"

"Wait a minute!" Jonas warned when he saw the guards reach for their weapons. "If you tell these men to do anything, someone is going to die!" The soft commanding note in his voice stopped the official's hand in mid-air. He hesitated, confused that he felt compelled to respond to the order of an apparent opium-dealer.

"Don't do anything yet," Jonas said. "The man wants me; that's the reason for the opium." He pointed toward the open crate and watched the customs official's indecision. "If you want to learn the truth, you had better keep this crowd calm." He turned to Martin, and, keeping his voice low, asked, "Where is Wong?"

Martin shrugged his shoulders helplessly. "I don't know," he replied, his eyes roaming from the right, across the doors leading out to the runways beyond. "There," he whispered, nudging Jonas. "There, beside the doors."

Jonas turned his head slowly to the left, being careful not to make any sudden moves that would trigger disaster. The first person he saw was Damrong standing with a tough-looking Chinese youth on his right and the man who must be Wong, Jonas' unsolicited enemy, on his left.

He glanced at Damrong again, sending a silent question about the young man's loyalty, and was satisfied with the unwavering look he received as a ghost of a smile flitted across his manager's somber face. No matter how questionable Damrong's actions had been in the past few weeks, Jonas knew he had not lost his allegiance.

Then he took a deliberately long, penetrating look at his opponent, measuring the man's cold, calculating look, his elegant appearance, his supreme self-confidence and ruthless amusement. Here was a man who would, by the snap of his fingers, send a man to his death and feel no regrets.

Neither man moved. Of all the people waiting in the terminal, these two were the most confident—one in the satisfactory conclusion of his evil plans; the other in his God.

As Jonas watched the man's cruel expression he knew he had to do something that would throw him off-balance. There had to be a weakness in his plan or his character that would save the situation, and Jonas intended to find it. Silently committing himself into the Lord's hands, Jonas decided to take the initiative.

Elizabeth had been watching him carefully and knew what he was about to do. Her hand flew out to stop him. "He'll kill you!" she whispered.

But Jonas' eyes were still on Wong, and he stepped around the crates and moved through the unresisting group of security guards who parted to let him through before fully realizing what he was intending to do.

He moved slowly toward his adversary; they met in the middle of an empty area between the group of security men and Damrong and his guard. The tension in the room intensified, but Jonas pushed the emotion from his mind, forcing his thoughts not to be hampered by the crowd's fear nor his own physical weakness.

"Well, Mr. Adams," Wong said in amusement as he folded his arms across his chest, "are you coming to beg for mercy?"

Jonas shook his head slowly, his eyes never leaving Wong's, his inner determination giving his thoughts a sharpness he had not often felt.

"Have I met you before, Mr. Wong? I don't understand this personal vendetta you seem to have for me."

Black oriental eyes turned hard for a moment. "We have met," Wong replied coldly. Then regaining his cold smile, he said, "Tell me, are you enjoying this meeting?"

"Not particularly," Jonas answered dryly, his eyes sweeping over the man's face significantly before he stared back into those hate-filled eyes.

"That's too bad," Wong smiled, understanding Jonas completely, but determined to provoke him into such agitation that he would lose his courage. "That's really too bad. It's going to become quite interesting soon."

Jonas raised his eyebrows doubtfully. "Perhaps. But tell me where we've met," he said as he looked over the man's shoulder to see Damrong attempting to edge away from his guard who was intently watching Wong and seemed unaware of anything else. "I don't recall ever having done any business with you, but perhaps we have?"

"No!" Wong replied, his voice sharp with fury. Jonas knew he had hit a nerve as he saw a little of the man's amusement slip away.

Jonas prodded again. "Are you sure?"

"Absolutely," the man replied in flawless English. "But we have met at your . . . clinic." His voice was full of accusation.

"And what happened then?" Jonas kept his face unreadable and emotionless as he stared hard at Wong.

"Your third-rate American doctors, in their usual

callous disregard for patients, killed my wife!''

"Oh, yes," Jonas replied softly, suddenly remembering the distressing scene Wong had created at the clinic. He had wondered then about the sincerity of Wong's protests. "I remember. You brought your wife into the clinic in the last stages of a tubercular condition and expected the doctors to perform a miracle."

Wong spoke scathingly. "I thought you worshipped a God of miracles. You could have saved her," he spat out acrimoniously, beginning to lose control of his emotions. "But you let her die, and now you're going to pay for it!"

"*You* let her die," Jonas corrected quietly, "because you waited too long to bring her in. You *were* warned, as I recall. Why didn't you do anything? Was it because you didn't really want to help her? Because you were using your poor wife to trap an American?"

Jonas was purposely goading Wong, hoping to provoke him into anger so that he would no longer be able to use that scheming, devious mind of his. He knew it was a dangerous game, for if he pushed too far, there could be a lot of blood spilled in that room within a matter of minutes. But now that he had Wong a little upset, he wanted to try one more subject; it just might be what was needed.

He smiled slightly, startling the Chinese, and then said, "What are your plans, now that you've got me arrested?"

Wong narrowed his gaze suspiciously and answered sharply, "I'm leaving the country. Do you see that plane that has just taxied up out there?" he asked, indicating the exit doors behind him. "My pilot is waiting for me."

"And where are you going?"

Wong's expression said that he thought that wasn't any of Jonas' business, but he snapped, "To Singapore." Then he added spitefully, "I'm sorry I can't stay around to see you shot. You know it won't take much to incite these people against you."

"Perhaps," Jonas said in wry amusement, "but I suggest that you leave before the police arrive."

"Why?" Wong was beginning to understand that his opponent was very perceptive, and this forced him into responding in a way he never intended. Knowing it was dangerous to stay, he still felt compelled to reverse his decision. "I believe I should stay to give the police all the information I have on your activities."

"No," Jonas smiled, "I don't think you'll want to wait."

Irritation sharpened Wong's voice and he reached absent-mindedly into his pocket and drew out an ugly-looking knife which, Jonas noticed with a great deal of interest, had a small red tiger on the handle. "Why shouldn't I stay?" Wong asked.

"Because the police know that . . ." Jonas paused, as a sudden inspiration hit him, "you're the Red Tiger." This brought a startled reaction from Wong but Jonas continued, "They've set a trap for you," and mentally apologized to Prince Chandruang if that wasn't exactly the truth.

"How do they know that?" Wong's hand tightened on the knife; he didn't even attempt to deny Jonas' statement.

"I should think that's obvious—they've planted an informer among your people." Jonas didn't know this for a fact, but, in glancing up again, saw that Damrong had moved a few feet away from his guard and was intently looking for a place to hide. This action underscored his suspicions of what Damrong had been doing the last few weeks.

Jonas wasn't prepared for what happened next—for he had just been making a wild guess—but Wong had someone in mind and turned to bark out an order at the young Chinese behind him. Before anyone could stop him, the young man whipped out a gun from his coat pocket and, turning his head, pulled the trigger.

Damrong made a quick, desperate move to get out of the way, throwing himself toward some crates stacked along the wall, but he was a second too late. The force of the bullet shot from such close range spun his body around and he hit the crates so hard they cracked. Clutching his stomach, he crumpled helplessly to the floor.

In the next second another shot rang out, this time from one of the security men, and Wong's guard dropped the gun he had just used on Damrong, clutched his chest with both hands, and collapsed to the floor.

There was instant pandemonium in the building. Those who had been watching so silently and eagerly from around the room began to shout in protest and fear and ran, like frightened forest monkeys, for cover.

Just as Wong's gunman fired his shot, Jonas shouted, "No, don't!" and tried to run to Damrong, but Wong thrust his knife out threateningly and brought him to a sudden stop. "Don't move!" he warned.

Elizabeth sobbed in horror, and, ignoring Martin's restraining hand and the guns ready to strike again when ordered, ran to the place where Damrong lay, blood seeping through his shirt, and knelt down to see if he was still alive.

At that same moment sirens were heard outside announcing the arrival of the police; the noise was a catalyst that propelled Wong into action. He threw an arm around Jonas' neck and pulled tightly, bringing him back against his own body as a shield. With the other hand, he pushed the knife up in front of Jonas' chest, forcing him to move back toward the exit doors.

"Don't move, or this man will be killed!" he shouted in Thai.

A security guard, thinking he could do something, made a move toward his gun, but Wong thrust the knife out to verify his words.

"I meant it! I'll slit his throat if anyone makes another move!"

Instantly, the room was stilled. The drama being played out was painfully real, and it was as though one single breath had been drawn by all of the observers as they watched the two men move nearer the exit doors.

As if on cue, the police burst upon the scene from the opposite side of the room, but were stopped instantly by a security guard who warned them softly in Thai of what was taking place. They stood helpless—unable to come to Jonas' aid, unable to exert their authority, impotent against the knife at Jonas' chest—and so joined the rest of those who could do nothing but watch Wong make a safe escape.

Jonas took one last glance at Elizabeth as she knelt on the floor beside Damrong, staring up at him in anguish. Pouring all of his emotions into the look that passed between them, he couldn't say what was in his heart, but if he was about to die, he wanted her to know his feelings. Elizabeth knew she was looking right into his soul, seeing for the first time in her life the deep, immeasurable love a man could have for her, and she whispered his name, too shaken to do anything but answer his look with an honest response.

"Jonas," she cried softly, her voice breaking. "Oh, Lord, help! Please, help us!"

A slight smile touched his lips and then he was jerked through the doors and out toward the waiting aircraft.

He felt Wong's breath on his neck; it came in convulsive spasms, and meant the man was running a little scared. Wong shifted his hold to grasp Jonas by the arm, and, holding the knife to his back, and moved with more speed around the tail of the plane. There, shielded by the aircraft, Wong shoved Jonas forward to the door.

"Get in!" he ordered, indicating the step on the strut.

"Hurry up!" He was extremely nervous and kept glancing around for any police or security guards who might have gotten behind them.

Jonas reluctantly reached for the door handle, swung it open and pulled himself up into the front seat, deliberately leaving himself free of the seat belt in case he ended up in a fight for his life.

A moment later Wong was sitting behind him, opening a briefcase that lay on the seat beside him. Jonas heard the case click open, and sneaked a look over his shoulder to see the Chinese pull a gun from its interior.

"Richards," he said, looking at the pilot as he shut the briefcase, "get this thing out on the runway, and let's get out of here."

Jonas turned in surprise to remind Wong that they couldn't just take off without clearance. There were too many planes coming in and out of the airport, and when he glanced at the pilot to lodge a protest he had another surprise. The man was English—perhaps an adventurer or a pilot who had, for one reason or another, lost his license and couldn't fly in his home country.

"What are you doing here?" Jonas asked.

"Makin' a livin'," the pilot growled.

"With *this* crook? Just how long do you expect your luck to last with him?"

But Richards didn't have opportunity to answer for Wong interrupted them angrily.

"Shut up, both of you! I want this plane in the air—now!"

The pilot turned in protest. "Wait a minute, I've got to get ground clearance first. There's a lot of traffic today."

"Do it!" The crazed look in Wong's eyes told the pilot he wasn't going to back down, and Richards, shrugging his shoulders in submission, reached for the microphone and informed ground control that they were taking off immediately, using the runway directly ahead.

"You're crazy," Jonas argued. "We'll never make it through the traffic."

As if to support his words, a commercial jet came screeching down the runway, passed their position by what seemed like just a few yards, and came to a halt to their left.

Ground control wasn't in support of Wong's decision either. The overhead speaker crackled with static as a voice spilled out into the aircraft.

"Eagle 13957 Sahara, this is ground control! You are to return to the tie-down area, return to the terminal immediately! Do not proceed to the runway! Return to your starting point immediately!"

Wong leaned forward to put the gun to the pilot's head. Richards stiffened for a second, then picked up the microphone.

"I've got a man holding a gun at my head. Clear out the traffic because we're going up."

"You're mad, Wong, absolutely mad," Jonas muttered under his breath. He leaned forward to scan the runway, then searched the sky around them. He shook his head, not believing they could avoid crashing into some unsuspecting aircraft that was coming in for a landing.

The speaker came alive again, warning all aircraft of an emergency and instructing them to stay clear of the airport until further notice. During these instructions, the pilot had taxied out to the runway and began to brake for a stop.

"What are you doing?" Wong demanded nervously.

"I need to go through my pre-takeoff," Richards replied, glancing at Jonas to let him know he was trying to stall for time, perhaps hoping ground control could clear the traffic better.

"You should have done that before you started this thing," Wong responded, ignoring the necessity for checking out the plane before continuing on to the runway. "Get going!"

Once again Richards shrugged his shoulders in resignation, and pressing the starboard rudder pedal, taxied out on the runway. Then, with a dubious glance at Jonas, he pushed the throttle all the way in and began his takeoff. The plane picked up speed and within a few seconds the pounding of the wheels stopped and they lost contact with the ground.

All during this time, ground control had been continuously warning other aircraft in the vicinity of their traffic pattern. The voice sounded as tense as Jonas felt, and he waited for a sudden, crunching impact, not for one moment believing they would make it into the air without harm.

Suddenly, off to their left, he saw another plane attempting to pull out of this flight pattern.

"Look out!" he called over the sound of the engine, pointing out their danger, and holding his breath as the other aircraft nosed up hard. Involuntarily, he ducked when it roared over their heads, missing them by less than the plane's width.

He glanced at the pilot whose face was grim. "You must have a lucky charm on you," Richards said, putting the plane into a steep climb. "I want to get as high as possible as soon as I can." He was aiming for the bay, gaining all the altitude he could to get away from the city, and in less then two minutes they were over the water.

Richards slumped back in his seat. "Singapore, here we come," he said with a jauntiness that announced his relief that they had made it that far without mishap. He settled back to maintain a climb.

Wong's next instructions jerked him out of his momentary satisfaction, and Jonas, who had not been able to relax at all, was equally stunned. Both men turned to stare over their shoulders at the man behind them.

"We're not going to Singapore. Head for Hong Kong."

"What?" the pilot asked. "What in the world are . . ."

"You heard me. Hong Kong," Wong said threateningly.

"But we can't! I filed flight plans for Singapore. And besides, we don't have enough fuel to take us that far."

"You should have seen to that," Wong spit out.

"How could I? You demanded that I get the plane up to the terminal immediately, not even giving me time to check it out. Remember? I didn't have enough time to get this thing filled up. I warned you, but you wouldn't listen!"

"Stop making excuses and do what I tell you." Wong's anger was beginning to spill over again; his voice shook with rage, his hand began to tremble and the gun wavered. *He's going beyond reason,* Jonas thought. *There's no telling what he might decide to do next.*

In the air terminal, pandemonium broke out once again. Just as soon as Wong and Jonas disappeared into the plane, voices rose into a crescendo of frenzied agitation; Elizabeth had to call out several times to get attention for Damrong. And the noise got even louder as people crowded nearer, curious to see if the two men lying on the floor were dead or alive. Several guards ran out the door, hoping to stop the escape, while two policemen began making arrangements to transport Damrong to the hospital. He came to just as he was lifted from the floor.

"Jonas?" he questioned, barely moving his lips. "What happened to Jonas?"

"Don't worry," Martin answered reassuringly. "Just hang in there, Damrong. You're going to the hospital. Everything will be fine."

But Damrong had passed out again and hadn't heard all of Martin's attempt at encouragement.

As Damrong and Wong's guard were carried through the gaping crowd, Martin turned to the police captain standing beside them and asked, "Could you please get us in to ground control? I'm Jonas Adams' personal pilot. I'm sure there is something I could do to help, if I could hear what that plane is doing."

The captain looked skeptically at Martin and then at Elizabeth. It was her tormented expression that led him to acquiesce. "Come," he said, jerking his chin toward the tower. "I cannot promise, but I will try to get you in there."

It took several minutes of strong persuasion on the captain's part to convince ground control that Martin and Elizabeth should enter their private sphere of responsibility, but finally the two Americans were inside the room, listening for any transmissions that might come from Wong's plane.

Several attempts to raise a response from the plane failed, and Eliabeth turned to Martin in fear.

"Suppose it's crashed into the sea? Suppose Wong pushed Jonas out of the plane? What if . . ."

"Sh," Martin responded gently, putting a comforting arm around her shoulders. "Don't let your mind go on like that, Liz. Wong probably won't allow the pilot to contact us. They've only been up a few minutes."

"We have the plane on radar," someone announced.

"What direction?" Martin asked, moving nearer the screen.

"South, south west."

Elizabeth took a chair offered her and leaned her head back against the wall, eyes closed and mind racing through dreadful scenes that might be going on in that plane. Suppose Wong has killed Jonas!

Jonas wasn't dead, but he had no fanciful notions about his chances of getting out of the situation alive. The mood inside the aircraft was one of tense fury—the unpredictable kind that could bring sudden and violent death.

The pilot turned around to glare at Wong. "If you want to get to Hong Kong, then fly the plane yourself, you crazy . . ."

Jonas tried to interrupt the growing argument before the two men came to blows. "Wong, it makes more sense to . . ."

But his opponent wasn't interested in advice. "Shut up, or I'll dump you out right here! How would you like a swim in the Gulf of Thailand—if you're still alive by the time you hit the water." Then he turned his attention back to the pilot. "I'll kill you if you don't do what I say!"

Jonas saw the gun raised between the two front seats so that it rested just inches from the pilot's head and heard Wong's voice, closer now that he had leaned forward to make his threats.

It was the opportunity he had been waiting for, perhaps the only one he would have to try to gain his freedom. With one single thought winging heavenward for help, he reached out with both hands to grab Wong's wrist, clamping down hard and pulling forward. It threw Wong off-balance, with a surprised snarl he fell against the front seat, then braced himself and began pulling against Jonas.

The two men were locked in a battle for the gun. Sitting in the front seat, Jonas was at a great disadvantage—at times almost fighting Wong at his back, at times twisted around with a foot braced against the door of the plane. He tried to keep the gun away from the pilot, not wanting it to go off and hit him, but he didn't have much control over what direction it was aimed. Using one hand, he pushed the gun to the right and up, so that he could break Wong's hold on the trigger, and nearly succeeded—until

Wong braced a knee on the back of Jonas' seat and broke free enough to regain his grip.

No one spoke, but Jonas was dimly aware of anxious looks from the pilot as he tried to keep out of the way while maintaining control of the plane. There wasn't much room for such a struggle—it was like boxing in a shower stall—but Jonas knew he couldn't wait passively to die.

He strained to keep Wong on the defensive, fighting as aggressively as he could. He jammed Wong's hand against the seat and could feel the man's grip loosening.

The gangster's arm jerked hard to the left, surprising Jonas; the gun pointed upward slightly and then, it went off with a sickening explosion.

Jonas saw the pilot lunge forward and heard him yell a savage oath, then slump to the left in his seat, his foot jamming the rudder and causing the plane to bank a little to the left.

With a sudden burst of anger that Richards had been hit, Jonas gave one powerful wrench, pulling Wong's shoulder in between the seats, forcing the gun to go off again.

The Chinese struggled to get out, one hand pushing against the seat, the other relaxing its grip on the gun. Before Jonas lost his advantage, he slammed one side of a hand down on Wong's neck, jerked the gun free, and, before Wong could move, hit him on the head, knocking him unconscious.

Swiftly, he reached into Wong's pocket and pulled out the knife he had used, stowed both weapons out of reach, then pushed Wong's body back through the opening and let him fall to the floor.

He sat a moment, gasping for breath, stunned at the way he had responded so violently. One of the first things he ought to do, he thought wryly, if he got back to Bangkok in one piece, was to take some lessons in the martial arts—in case this was going to become a new life style.

Then he turned to look at the pilot.

Richards' head was bleeding from above his ear and across the hairline; the bullet must have grazed his head. Jonas didn't know how deep the wound was, but he saw that Richards was in no condition to fly the plane. He reached down to pull the pilot's foot off the rudder, and found it difficult to get his leg propped up in such close quarters. But he didn't want him hitting the rudders again.

He took a quick look to see what the aircraft's position was and reached for the microphone.

"Ground control, this is Eagle 13957 Sahara. The pilot has been shot and is unconscious. What do I do now?"

He made an effort to keep his voice calm and impersonal, but he was still trying to get his breath back, and the immediate need of getting the plane down on his own made his voice tremble.

Every head in the ground control room swiveled toward the speaker as they heard this announcement. Elizabeth sat straight up in the chair and stared at Martin. She didn't know if Jonas could fly a plane, and was worried about what Wong might be doing. It was horrible just sitting there unable to control the hopelessly deteriorating situation around her.

Martin asked for permission to talk with Jonas and sat down before the instruments as calmly as though he were going to have a nice long visit over the telephone with a friend.

"Jonas, this is Martin. Are you OK?"

"That's a welcome voice," Jonas responded in relief, feeling as though he were sitting on a space rocket and burning a hole in the tropical blue sky. "I'm all right, Martin."

"What's happened to Wong?"

"He's unconscious."

"I'd like to know how that happened," Martin said

with a smile at Elizabeth, who now stood nervously beside him. "Jonas, what's the attitude of the airplane?"

Jonas wasn't sure what Martin meant, but said, "We've been climbing ever since we left the airport, and we're in a gentle left turn."

"OK. Just sit back and relax. We'll get you down."

Jonas grunted. *Relax,* he thought. *That was easy for Martin to say; he knows planes like he knows the back of his hand!*

"I've always wanted to learn to fly, but this isn't exactly the way I planned to do it," he said into the microphone.

"You'll do fine, Jonas," Martin said, trying to help his employer relax. "All you need to do is follow my instructions. Do you know where the throttle is?"

"Yes," Jonas replied. He had sat at the controls enough that he knew most of the instruments, but had never really tried to fly, usually spending most of his time working on business papers or visiting with passengers.

"OK. Pull the throttle back towards you a little," Martin instructed. "The nose will come down. Then push the control yoke forward just a little, until the nose lines up with the horizon. If you can use the horizon indicator, that will help."

Very gingerly, Jonas followed Martin's instructions and sighed in relief when the plane responded just as Martin had said. Then he reported what had been done.

Martin's voice came back reassuringly. "Great. We'll make a pilot out of you yet, Jonas. Now, do you know where the tachometer is? It's probably showing about 26. Pull the throttle back until it reads 22—that's low cruise. The air speed indicator should show about 90 knots."

Jonas looked over to the instruments Martin had mentioned, stared at them a minute, and then pushed the button down on the microphone.

"Martin, a bullet smashed the air speed indicator—it's inoperative."

There was silence from the overhead speaker for a few seconds, and Jonas felt panic curling up in his stomach.

Elizabeth saw Martin's grip on the microphone tighten and it frightened her. Did this mean the plane would crash?

"Martin?" she asked, touching his arm.

"It's OK, Liz."

"But if the pilot was wounded by gunshot, what condition is Jonas in?" she asked frantically.

Martin didn't reply, but his voice went out soothingly over the microphone. "Don't worry, Jonas. We can do without the air speed indicator. Just pull back on the throttle about one inch."

Jonas obeyed the instruction, but he was still heading out over the gulf. His mind screamed at him to return immediately to the airport, but he forced his mind and hands to be patient, to follow Martin's words. It was the only way he was going to get back without crashing.

"Jonas, we've got you on radar. You're heading southwest over the bay. What we want you to do now is to find the magnetic compass; it's up above the instrument panel. What does it read?"

"230 degrees," Jonas responded tersely.

"OK. Use the control yoke and turn slowly to the left. When the compass reads 50 degrees, roll the yoke back to a level flight."

In a few moments, Jonas looked out to see the city of Bangkok in the distance, and as it came slowly toward him, he began following Martin's instructions to turn the control yoke to the left and right by ten and twenty degree increments. They were lining him up to come straight at the airport.

"What altitude do you have, Jonas?"

He looked at the altimeter on the pilot's side of the instrument panel. "It reads 20."

"OK," Martin's voice returned cheerfully. "What I

want you to do now is to pull the throttle back a little until the tachometer reads 20.''

Jonas followed the instructions, but the altimeter dropped to 18. When he radioed this information to Martin, he was assured it was no problem.

"Can you see the runway, Jonas?"

"Yes, I'm almost on top of it."

"Good. Now pull the throttle back a little, about another inch. Pull back on the yoke, until you've cut your speed down."

"Right." Jonas pulled the throttle back but saw the ground coming at him faster than he liked; he forced himself to concentrate on following Martin's instructions to the letter.

Just as he reached the threshold of the runway, Martin cut through the static again. "You're looking great, Jonas. Maintain that speed. You've got a lot of runway to work in, so don't worry."

The plane dipped down close to the runway and Jonas didn't know what he should do. "Now what, Martin?"

"Keep pulling back slowly on the yoke and use both rudder pedals to maintain a straight course. You're doing fine. You'll be down in a minute, Jonas."

Suddenly, Jonas felt the wheels touch the ground and saw the nose of the plane sink a little.

Martin's voice came over the speaker, jubilantly. "You've done it, Jonas! Sit tight and let it roll to a stop."

Jonas pushed the button on the microphone for one last time. "We need an ambulance right away," he said, glancing over to see the pilot make a weak attempt to sit up before passing out again. "It's all right, Richards. We're down," he said. "Thank you Lord!"

For what seemed like an unbearably protracted time, the plane rolled down the runway and Jonas was beginning to wonder if he would have to crash into something to get it stopped.

He glanced over his shoulder when he heard a moan from Wong, hoping he wouldn't have to deal with him again, then looked back out the windshield to discover that they had finally rolled to a stop. With a heart full of gratitude to God, he reached over and cut the engine.

Taking a quick look once more at Wong stirring to consciousness and at the wounded pilot, whose face and neck seemed covered with blood, Jonas picked up the knife and gun, opened the door and crawled out of the plane.

Three police jeeps came racing up just as he stepped to the ground, and he ducked under the wing to be greeted by an elated Martin.

"You did it, Jonas!" Martin cried joyfully, throwing away his calm, placid nature as he gave his employer a bear hug.

"*You* did it," Jonas corrected, grinning at his pilot. "I owe you my life. Saying thanks isn't enough."

Martin smiled, shaking off his part of the adventure. "How about some flying lessons?" he teased.

"The first week you're on the job," Jonas replied banteringly, his eyes now on the young woman who stood beside the jeep, nervously clasping and unclasping her hands.

She was waiting for him, too reticent now that he was safe and looking at her with such a possessive expression, too embarrassed as she thought of the horrible things she had said to him, and even too fearful as she realized that she could be opening herself up to more pain and rejection.

But he took the initiative. Handing the two weapons to one of the police, and leaving them to take care of the two men in the plane, he moved slowly toward her, savoring the knowledge of what was to grow between them.

Then he stood before her, a heart-shattering tenderness on his face, and silently touched her cheek with his fingertips, as though he needed reassurance that she was really there.

"Welcome home," she whispered, her voice breaking as tears filled her eyes and caught at her throat.

They were suspended in their own bright world of discovery, totally unaware of the arrival of an ambulance, of one jeep leaving with Wong as a prisoner, and of the men still milling about them as they prepared to get men, jeeps and plane off the runway and out of the way of incoming aircraft.

Jonas smiled. "It's taboo to touch a woman in public in Thailand, let alone kiss her, but . . ." He reached out to take her in his arms, and in that moment, their private little world was shattered by a voice.

"I'm sorry, Sir." A short, black-haired Thai policeman stood beside Jonas, clearing his throat nervously, knowing he was interrupting something very special. "We must clear the field immediately, Sir. Other planes are waiting to land."

With a smile at Elizabeth and glint of promise in his eyes, Jonas nodded and turned to help her into the jeep. "Of course. We'd like to get to the hospital immediately and see my manager."

Martin called out to them as he swung himself up into the plane. "Jonas, I'm going to get this off the runway. I'll take the van that Damrong drove to the airport and meet you both later."

Once back in the air terminal, Jonas spoke to the police captain, promising that they would see Prince Chandruang as soon as they had been to the hospital. He barely took time to see that his crates of merchandise were carried into a side room to await the authorities' attention.

"I'll work with the police in getting that opium taken care of," he said to a customs official as he strode through the room, his hand on Elizabeth's arm. He hurried her past the lines of customers now intent on business, having forgotten the excitement of the morning. Out through the front entrance and over to his car, he hardly gave Elizabeth time to put her feet on the ground.

He hadn't said a word to her since leaving the runway, and still silent, he helped her into the car, shut the door, went around to the driver's side and got in.

Elizabeth felt her heart pounding; the moment of decision was upon her and she was frightened. Even though she had made peace with God about the bitterness that had filled her life, she wasn't sure that she could open her heart to another man who might do the same thing Peter had done. She turned to face Jonas, expecting to be swept into his arms, her face showing her inner turmoil. But those fears were allayed somewhat when she saw him rest his head on his arms folded over the steering wheel and heard him begin to pray.

"Oh, Lord, You're so strong and powerful. Your arm is not shortened that it can't save." He paused and then went on with tears tinging his words. "You've shown yourself to be the true God. You've saved our lives from death, and You've brought us together. I thank You, with all my heart, I thank You."

He raised his head and turned to her. "Will you trust me, Elizabeth? Be part of me, be my love? I need you so very much."

Elizabeth's eyes overflowed at his plea and the tears fell down her cheeks, evidence of how much her heart had been moved by the humility of his prayer and the courage he had shown. But would he be gentle with her?

Through the open windows of the car came the distinctly oriental sound of music from the radio of an airport laborer, the languid sound of thudding drums and pinging cymbals.

Jonas smiled and reached out to take her hand. "Drums and cymbals—the music of romance to Thai young people.

Will you let me love you, Liz? I'll never hurt you, I promise.''

He reached out to draw her into his arms. ''Do you love me?'' he asked, the yearning in his look almost more than she could bear.

Very slowly, the questioning look in her eyes was replaced by a warm glow, and she nodded her head, not trusting her voice.

And, held close in his arms, she realized the long night had finally past. Gone was the danger of guns and life-threatening situations, and gone, too, was the long night of dark bitterness that had threatened to ruin her life.

God truly keeps His promises, she thought. *When you pass through the waters, I will be with you; and through the rivers, they shall not overflow you . . . for I am the Lord your God.*

''Marry me,'' he whispered, and then gave her that kiss his eyes had been promising ever since she had welcomed him home on the runway. It was a kiss that was at first so gentle that she wanted to cry, and then so fierce that she knew her future was sealed.

When she was finally able to talk, she looked up into his face and asked teasingly, ''I thought you said it was taboo to kiss in public?''

''Oh, it is,'' he grinned and then glanced up behind them. ''But, there's a van on either side of the car and one just pulled up behind us,'' he said, his eyes dancing with joy. ''I guess that means our situation is private enough for another kiss.''

And he took it.

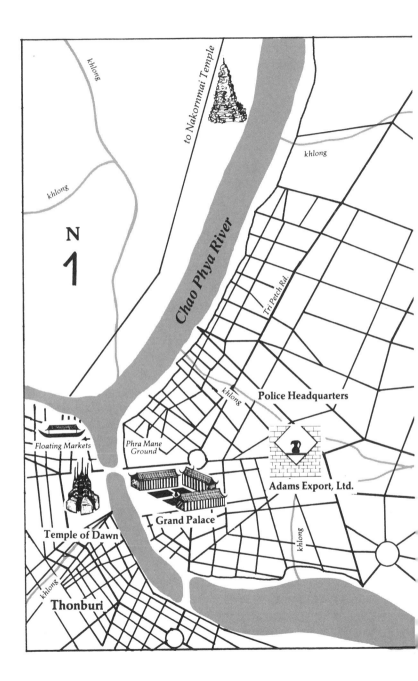

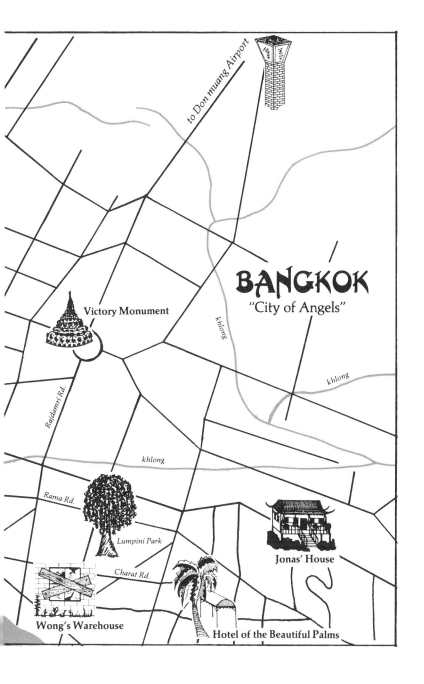

to Don muang Airport

BANGKOK
"City of Angels"

khlong

khlong

Victory Monument

Rajdamri Rd.

khlong

Rama Rd.

khlong

Lumpini Park

Jonas' House

Charat Rd.

Wong's Warehouse

Hotel of the Beautiful Palms